SWEET DARUSYA

A Tale Of Two Villages

Maria Matios

TRANSLATED FROM THE UKRAINIAN BY
MICHAEL M. NAYDAN
AND OLHA TYTARENKO

SPUYTEN DUYVIL
NEW YORK CITY

Library of Congress Cataloging-in-Publication Data

Names: Matios, Mariiã, 1959-author | Naydan, Michael M., 1952-
translator | Tytarenko, Olha, translator.
Title: sweet darusya : a tale of two villages/ Maria Matios
Description: New York City : Spuyten Duyvil, [2019]
Identifiers: LCCN 2019001826| ISBN 9781947980938
Subjects: Solodka Darusiã--Translations into English.
Classification: LCC PG3949.23.A814 S6513 2019
LC record available at https://lccn.loc.gov/2019001826

MARIA MATIOS
CHRONICLER OF THE CARPATHIAN PAST

Maria Matios was born in the village of Roztoky in the Bukovyna region of Ukraine in 1959 and is one of the most prolific and major prose writers in Ukraine today. She is from the post-independence generation of exciting new Ukrainian women writers who, instead of shunning their rural roots in postmodernist urbanized culture, like a Toni Morrison or Alice Walker in American culture, embraces those roots to give a voice to the past and to discover higher truths about themselves, their culture, and in the process, the human condition altogether.

Ms. Matios received her degree in philology at the University of Chernivtsi, and the first major publication of her prose was in the journal *Kyiv* in 1992. Since then she has authored twelve volumes of prose and seven books of poetry to date, focusing on prose for the past decade of her career. Her extensive list of published prose works includes: *A Nation* (2001), *Life is Short* (2001), *A Dime Store Novel* (2003), *A Smorgasbord from Maria Matios* (2003), *Sweet Darusya* (2004), *Diary of a Lost [Woman]* (2005), *Mr. and Mrs. U in Country UA* (2006), *A Nation: Revelations* (2006), *Almost Never Not the Opposite* (2007), *The Russky Lady. Momma Maritsa, the Wife of Christopher Columbus* (2008), *Culinary Tricks* (2009), *Four Seasons of Life* (2009), *Torn Pages from My Autobiography* (2010), *Armageddon already Happened* (2011), *Shoes of the Mother of God* (2013), and *A Private Diary. the*

Maidan. War... (2015). Her books of poetry include: *From Grass and Leaves* (1982), *The Fire of Turpentine* (1986), *The Garden of Impatience* (1994), *Ten Thresher Concaves of Ice Water* (1995), *A Woman's Lasso Dance* (2001), and *A Woman's Lasso Dance in the Garden of Impatience* (2007). She received the 2004 Book of the Year Award and the national Taras Shevchenko Prize in 2005 for her novel *Sweet Darusya,* and the grand Prize in the Crowning of the Word Competition for her novel *Almost Never Not the Opposite* (2007), which completes a trilogy of works based on her family chronicles and her life growing up in her Bukovyna Hutsul homeland in the Carpathians. The Hutsuls are the independent and colorful inhabitants of the Carpathian Mountains and were the subject of the famous film *Shadows of Forgotten Ancestors*, based on Mykhailo Kotsiubynsky's novella of the same name. Matios' novella *The Russky Lady* earned the book of the year award in 2008 in Ukraine. And her candid and often ironic memoir *Torn Pages from an Autobiography* (2010) received a book of the year award in Ukraine and recounts people and events in the Soviet Union and the transition to Ukrainian independence. Matios' fictional works are written in a savory writing style that captures the authentic indigenous dialect and cultural mores of the people from her native Bukovyna highlands.

On December 17, 2010 Matios reported that the offices of Piramida Publishers in Lviv were searched by members of the Ukrainian Ministry of Internal Affairs, who tried to remove copies of her autobiography from circulation.[1] The essence of the complaint against her book was the

---

1   An article in Ukrainska Pravda (The Ukrainian Truth) describes the situation in detail: http://www.pravda.com.ua/news/2011/01/12/5775945/.

fact that she called the gigantic titanium sword-wielding statue of the woman defender of the motherland in Kyiv a giant phallus.[2] Her comments apparently irked some Soviet army veterans of the "Great Patriotic War" (World War II), who made charges of defamation to the authoritarian Yanukovych government. Matios indignantly reacted to the illegal search with an open letter to the general procurator of Ukraine.[3] Apologies were extended to her, and there were no further repercussions. Matios currently resides in the capital city of Kyiv in Ukraine where, after the most recent free parliamentary elections that swept out the remains of the repressive Yanukovych regime, she is serving a second term as a deputy.

*

Sweet Darusya is a text with a great amount of texture and layers. The postcolonial masterpiece is an engaging character portrayal in the microcosmic world of a small village in Bukovyna. The villagers of *Sweet Darusya* speak the local Bukovynian dialect, which Matios extensively glosses with endnotes in the Ukrainian editions of the novel. While Matios's writing style is rich and complex, it is still quite accessible to the refined Ukrainian reader. Significantly, instead of disavowing rural stereotypes in her works, she revels in the unique individuality of her

---

2 A link to a picture of the monument can be found here: http://miraimages.photoshelter.com/image?&_bqG=2&_bqH=eJyriIgIMwnzqvLxDyv2SgoMj8ovCU9Ky8rKzE63MjIwsjI0MABhIOkZ7xLsbOuSm-paaV5yqBubFO_q52JYA2aHBrkHxni62oSCV3iWFhT75ERmhiaFq8Y7OIbb-FqYlFyRkA_MIhdA--&GI_ID=.

3   http://life.pravda.com.ua/columns/2011/01/12/70243/

ancestral villagers and shows their humanity as well as the psychological depth of their lives.

As though she were unpeeling an onion, Matios constructs her unique narrative in layers and in reverse chronological order. The primary narrator is a highly articulate one and close in sensibility to the omniscient author, though clearly an insider from that culture with an intrinsically deep understanding of it. On a second narrative layer two village women, one older and one younger, whose conversations are presented as asides, provide commentary on the events happening in the novel. They are local women of the *gazda* class (successful independent farmers) whose colorful language and commentary accompanying the events in the novel provide both a folksy philosophical depth and sometimes comic relief. This type of narration recalls Ukrainian writer Nikolai Gogol's narrator Rudy Panko from his collection of stories *Evenings on a Farm Near Dikanka*, which Boris Eikhenbaum has described as *skaz*. According to Nina Kolesnikoff in the *Encyclopedia of Contemporary Literary Theory*, "Eikhenbaum defined this kind of narration...as a special type of discourse oriented in its lexicon, syntax and intonation toward the oral speech of the narrator."[4] At the third level of narration one finds the actual characters interacting with each other in their own unique voices. These three narrative levels intertwine to tell the story of sweet Darusya and her family in reverse chronological order, with the time period closest to the present presented first, approximately in the 1960s, then the

---

4   Nina Kolesnikoff, "Formalism, Russian" in Irene Rima Makaryk, ed. *Encyclopedia of Contemporary Literary Theory: Approaches, Scholars, Terms* (Toronto: U of Toronto P, 1993): 55.

love relationship between sweet Darusya and Ivan Tsvychok that occurs prior to that time in the late 1940s and early 1950s, and finally the love relationship between Darusya's mother and father as well as Darusya's childhood in the 1930s and early 1940s. The reasons for this altered chronological order will become eminently clear to the reader upon completion of the novel. Not one to spoil the reader's anticipation, I leave that for the reader to discover. This kind of chronologically altered narrative has one of its most famous Slavic literary antecedents in Mikhail Lermontov's novel *A Hero of Our Time*, in which the reader comes to understand the psychological motivation of the hero Pechorin from earlier events, but only toward the very end.

Darusya, of course, at various stages and times in her life is at the core of the narrative of Matios' novel. The villagers euphemistically call her "sweet" so as not to call her "foolish" for her eccentric behavior and muteness. She is, in fact, somewhat of a combination of a traditional "holy fool" (*iurodivyi*) figure and a dervish. In the Eastern Slavic tradition holy fools are considered to be touched by God and sacred. Their seeming insanity is a mask in the world of human beings where they must dwell, while they are believed to be privy to higher truths in the spiritual realm. Darusya is also part dervish with her penchant for dancing alone in a circular motion in her need to escape the world of reality that causes her pain.

Most of the action in the novel occurs in two neighboring villages called Cheremoshne in the mysterious Carpathian Mountains on opposite sides of the Cheremosh River, which then marked the border between Romania and Ukraine (first under Polish rule, then later under the Soviets, and now in independent Ukraine after 1991). That part of the Carpathians is a land where life and magic intersect on a daily basis, where religion and folk beliefs intertwine and hold equal sway, where the plow of history all too often has torn lives asunder and destroyed innocent victims, of which sweet Darusya and her parents are but a few. The events unfolding in *Sweet Darusya* occur on the backdrop of true historical events and experiences that Matios draws from her family's own life, particularly World War II and the Soviet occupation of that region after the war. The novel, in fact, reads like an intimate family chronicle, one that accompanies the flow of a bloody history filled with senseless violence and inhumanity.

The novel, too, is one about a strong and proud indigenous people (the Hutsuls), who live hard, work hard, play hard, and love hard according to their traditional mores. Some of them also show their darker side in the novel: they lie, cheat, steal, have extramarital affairs, and envy their neighbors. While sweet Darusya and her spiritual love Ivan Tsvychok are nearly outcasts in that microcosmic society, they are the embodiment of truth that could set people free (if those people would only listen).

Sweet Darusya is in many respects a novel about trauma and higher truths. Matios presents that trauma on multiple levels from the micro- to the macrocosmic: from Darusya's own personal tragedy, to her family's, to the village's, and to the nation's. Darusya's innocence and way of life are destroyed, and her childhood taken away from her by forces from outside her village society. Yet she still must somehow learn to live and cope in that violated world with her emotional pain and suffering.

The translation tries to retain as much of the texture of the original as possible, but the incongruities of Ukrainian and English at times lead to certain concessions in favor of clarity in the latter. It also attempts to retain Matios' unique colloquial manner of expression, opting for the literal sometimes instead of just conveying idiomatic meaning. This at times will make the text sound less polished for an Anglophone reader. It is important to point out that the culture Maria Matios describes in the novel is a rural, agricultural one, geographically isolated in the Carpathian Mountains and caught between various occupying forces (the Poles, the Romanians, and the Soviet Russians) at different times. Therefore much of the language in the novel mirrors that multilingual character of the locality as well as the rustic way of life of times past.

*

SWEET DARUSYA

A TALE OF TWO VILLAGES

THE EVERYDAY DRAMA

"Where, Maria, who did you get the georginas[5] from that are so bright and puffy?" Vasyuta asked her neighbor over the fence. "No matter how hard I took care of mine, they were wiped out by some kind of disease. They became curled like snails; you can't do anything about it. Maybe I gave them to wicked people, or maybe Varvara plucked them out at night, it's not for me to say to you what kind of witch she might be. God only knows what happened to my flowers? They're gone—and you can't do anything about it. And this weed is useless. I love it when flowers are big and puffy, and not teeny tiny," and she throws out an armful of asters onto the path.

"Fie on such a miracle! Everybody's asking who'd you get them from, who'd... they'll hex my harvest," Maria answers without straightening herself up from the garden bed as though she were angry. "It was sweet Darusya who gave them to me. Both the lilacs and the rose bushes. She brought them to me in the spring."

"Before things got bad with her again?"

"No-no, it was already after that. She, poor orphan, carried around the dug up roots all over the village as if they were her child. She wrapped them up in a blanket she used to cover herself with, pressed them to her breasts to warm them up, and brought them—unswaddled them just like a child. I'm telling you, Vasyuta, my heart began to ache so much then that I thought twice about even quarreling with

---

5   Georgina (colloquial) means dahlias. In Bukovyna georgina isn't a Russian word. It's not even a woman's name. [author's note]

1

*my Slavko, and he's not handicapped after all... I wish light-
ning had struck him in my bosom, he'll make me die before
my time with that damned vodka of his, God grant he burn
up...."*

"May boils cover my tongue for saying such things!"

*

...And sweet Darusya is sitting in a flower bed among
the asters, three steps from Maria and Vasylyna, she's
braiding and unbraiding her hair that had thinned out
and turned gray long ago, she's listening to the tender
conversation about her, just quietly smiling to herself.

They just don't have any brains in their head or God
in their belly, her neighbors, 'cause they think she's foolish in the head. But Darusya's not foolish — she's sweet.

So what if she raked the dahlia roots into a blanket?
It was right at the time the snow had disappeared, and
the frost hadn't yet let up. Darusya passed the flowers
out throughout the village because she had dug up so
many in the spring, even more than there were potatoes
in the cellar. And so she carried them to the houses that
didn't have flowers blooming around them. Would she
have carried a bare root in such a chill? For some reason
Vasyuta doesn't carry her grandson to the garden in just
his pants, but wraps him up in a little blanket, and then
takes him in her arms and rocks him through the village.
A child is just like a living flower.

Darusya is sitting on the warm, still almost summery
ground, she's stroking the cheery little heads of the asters, with the palm of her hand she's tousling the fragrant

locks, speaking to them, telling them what she wants, laughing — and what is so foolish about that?

How can she be foolish when she *understands* everything, she knows what everything is called, what today's date is, how many apple trees have borne fruit in Maria's garden, how many people have been born in the village from one Christmas to another, and how many have died?! In the Village Council they look up this kind of knowledge in a book, but Darusya keeps everything in her head. She's better off talking to chickens than to people. The trees understand her, dogs don't bother her, but people — no. People can't leave Darusya alone.

But she doesn't want to talk to people, because then they'll just *give her a piece of candy* they know will make her sick.

And what can you think about this when there's nothing to think about? People in the village sometimes do things that even make Darusya tear her hair out, but for some reason they don't call them foolish, but about her, who speaks with the trees and flowers, and who just lives the way she wants, and though she doesn't do any harm to anyone, they think of her as foolish.

And if she's really foolish, can you tell she's handicapped by looking at her?

...Fedyo put a saddle on his ram and carried his son to school on it, and no one said that Fedyo was foolish, though from that day on, the nickname "ram-boy" stuck to his son.

And Stepan one day came from the city on the village church's feast day celebration and brought with him a shiny round washer of immense proportion. Near the club the boys were playing "dare," and Stepan bet a bottle of beer he could put the steel washer onto the foolishness under his pants, and after half an hour remove it, with no harm done to his foolishness. But the foolishness from under Stepan's pants didn't take heed of Stepan, swelled up, and nearly broke off in the skirmish with the washer. So Dmytro the welder ended up cutting off the washer on Stepan's shame with some kind of saw. It took so long that his hands shook because he didn't want to cause damage to Stepan's goods, because Stepan was supposed to get married soon. They laughed it up in the village, lamented a bit — but they forgot to call Stepan foolish.

In the village they think Darusya doesn't understand, so they use the word *sweet* in talking to her instead of calling her *foolish*.

Maria's son Slavko somehow once got so drunk that he carried out an entire yearling pig, stabbed it thirteen times in the chest with a knife, threw it into the pond near the house, and banned his household from going up to the water. "Let the damn bastard swim!" The drunken Slavko screamed so loudly that he could be heard countywide. "And whoever doesn't do it my way will be catching frogs in the pond!" The pig floated for two days in the water, and it was really getting to be a hot summer, so it started to stink, and no one of Slavko's household dared take pity on the mortified soul, fearful of the crazed drunken temper of the master of the house.

But it was Darusya who waited things out until his entire household had gone their separate ways. She took a pitchfork, found a new rope for the cow in Slavko's barn, brought a stone from the river, carried the pig to the banks with the pitchfork, tied a stone around it, made a sign of the cross over it—and the poor killed thing began to gurgle its way to the bottom.

In the evening Slavko stormed in the yard and roared like a bull across the fence at Darusya, baring his rotten teeth:

"Fool!!! Fool, don't you want a candy? Here's a candy for you! A candy!" And he threw a handful of barberry flavored ones right near the door to her house.

*

It would have been better if he had not mentioned the *candy*. In the village no person with half a brain mentions or gives Darusya candies: they know that her head aches from *sweets* and she vomits terribly from them. So terribly that by morning not even a tiny sliver of life remains in her. And it takes her a week to come back from that other world.

It happened that way after Slavko's words.

Darusya didn't leave the house for two days—her head ached so much that she couldn't even look at the ceiling, she just tied her head up with scarves, covered herself up with a pillow and turned away toward the wall. She didn't eat, didn't drink, didn't get up to go to the bathroom—she just waited until the iron rings that were pressing her head broke, as if they had wanted to completely crush her.

A few times Maria took a look in on Darusya. She silently put a half-liter of milk on the table, and then she unwrapped Darusya's head and rubbed it in badger fat.

On the top she put on a cabbage leaf, onto the leaf—a small handful of coarse wool and tied it up again with a white scarf.

Darusya, wasted away, quite entirely without strength, dwindled like a little child, silently let herself be turned over, and then sat down, holding her head in her lap until Maria rubbed badger fat on the crown of her head with her cold hands. She didn't have the strength to say a word. Her head had been blown off somewhere so far away that she held it all the more tightly with her hands as though she were defending herself from a thug. If that thug would have been so kind as to call some butcher, maybe Semén, who chops up pigs for people, and if Semén could have cut out the pain from Darusya's head, then she would have been overjoyed, and, maybe, finally would have begun to speak.

But the thug was nowhere to be seen, just a sharp unbearable knife tears along under the crown of her head— and from despair Darusya at that very moment would have given her head to be chopped off. She doesn't have the strength to endure that infinite pain. She doesn't have the strength even to listen as Maria quietly sobs at the table and sniffles. It would have been better for her to go to her Slavko or to anybody she wanted to go to, so the sobbing would not torment her. Maria's sobbing seems like the blows of a hammer in a gypsy forge. And Darusya all the more strongly presses against the wall, yearning for just peace and quiet.

It was this way every time when the pain knocked her down. Maria, crying a little and grumbling inaudible words under her nose, walked on further. And Darusya remained with her head ripped apart from the pain in an empty house until *something* hit her like a knife in the heart—and then she got up and went where her eyes led.

*

...And this time her legs carried her to the river. Darusya went into the water up to her knees—and she felt better right away. The cold water floated through her somewhere to the very edge of the sky, and with eyes shut Darusya rocked side-to-side, sensing the rings that had been pressing her head for two days and nights had loosened up. Somewhere there, deep inside, they cracked so loudly that it seemed like sparks were strewing themselves into the river, but Darusya didn't open her eyes, knowing that, just as she opens them, the rings again will plait a nest in her poor little head, the way that snakes on the Feast of the Holy Cross wind their lair into the ground for the winter.

When Darusya's head hurts, she has to wade into the river up to her waist. Otherwise the pain cuts her into tiny little pieces. It's good during the summer when the water is warm. Then no one forbids her from standing in it. When it turns cold, she goes into the water just up to her knees. The colder the water, the quicker the pain would let go of Darusya.

The first time after having attacks of pain for several days, something told Darusya that she needed to look for *cold water*. At first she looked for a long time into the well in her yard. But it was far down to the water, and Darusya didn't have a long ladder. The one that led to the chicken coop had rotted long ago and wouldn't reach the bottom. Then Darusya stumbled to the river, with both of her hands holding her head as if at any moment it might roll off her neck, with her drunken gait frightening the village women in their flowerbeds and vegetable gardens. While she was slowly entering the water in her bare feet, nearly half of the neighborhood gathered.

"Mother of God, she's come to drown herself! Tie her up, Maria, she'll only let you come up to her!" Varvara the thief said to Darusya's neighbor from the riverbank, waving a twisted rope from the wash line.

Maria looked for a long time as Darusya with eyes shut rocked from side to side, having gone up to her chest into the icy water. Quietly she finally said:

"Leave her be, girls... She won't do anything to herself. As God grants, so it will be. And you don't have to tie her up, Varvara. It's better if you tie up your tongue with that rope... Go back to your homes, ladies, and I'll sit a bit near sweet Darusya and then I'll go home to my stupid...."

*

Since that time no one would go with Darusya to the river any more. She wouldn't even have gone there if she didn't have to rinse her wash. But wash is wash, your head is more important. So, when just after the attacks of pain something drove her out of bed, she would go to the river, and no one held her arms anymore; the women just followed her movements with their eyes, placing their palms over their brows, and one of the school children quietly chuckled: "Just look, sweet Darusya is going swimming again." For that time and again he got a poke in the back of the neck from another schoolboy who was a little more intelligent than he was.

It's good until the river freezes up. And the first time that Darusya stood on the ice and it didn't break, she wanted to break it with her head because she needed to go into the icy water, even if it would have cost her her life. She got down on her knees, hit her brow once or twice on the ice—and quietly began to whimper: the ice was hard and didn't give in. Darusya stamped her bare feet along the river's frozen floor, her legs weakened from several days of lying down, she struck the ice as though she were kneading clay, and wrung her hands from despair.

And here from somewhere, as if he were following in her footsteps, Maria's Slavko appeared. And Darusya's head immediately stopped hurting: *Slavko was sober.* It seemed to her that since birth—perhaps only during childhood—she hadn't seen Slavko sober, and now he was steadily walking to her to the middle of the river with a trembling outstretched hand. Always with a mouth full of words, Slavko this time was as silent as a mute.

And Darusya also stretched out her hand to him.

So they walked along the bank, with hands stretched out to one another, as though they were being led to a marriage ceremony or on a rope leash. Slavko didn't utter a cutting—or any—word for that matter, and Darusya obediently followed him, not feeling the wintry cold.

Slavko brought Darusya to the village greenhouse. A small, almost round little lake with a handful of fountains that were unceasingly pulsing up from under the earth hid behind the fence of bare willows by the bank. The clean water pulsed in front of Darusya's eyes, and she, immodestly rolling her skirt up to her bellybutton, stepped into the abundant gurgling.

When she stepped onto the bank, Slavko wasn't anywhere to be seen. But she knew the way home herself.

*

...So now Darusya is standing in the cold bath of autumn—and fighting with the nails hammered into her head by some kind of heavy, heartless hammer. A certain amount of time passes—the black iron of pain finally settles on the river bottom, and then spreading one of her headscarves, Darusya sits down on a stone. The pure transparent water rinses her bare legs and further down all the way to her ankles. She feels it finally easing for her. The gurgling of the river finally calms Darusya—and again she returns to her endless thinking.

She doesn't know how not to think. Perhaps it's because she doesn't say a word to anyone, but isn't mute, that's why she thinks incessantly. So she thinks about everything in the world—and from that her head is always aching.

...Darusya is surprised that no one ties up Slavko when he gets drunk and debauches all over half the village. On Easter Sunday he got so loaded that he wanted to burn down the barn, and then a blue flame shot out of his mouth.

Her head uncovered,[6] Maria ran to her neighbors screaming and crying: "Good people, help! Christ is Risen! Slavko's dying!"

Mykola the forester, without getting up from the Easter table, peacefully told the disheveled Maria, who looked like a madwoman standing at the doorway: "Maria, piss into his mouth, he'll get better right away. If you don't have any piss, dilute some horse dung with water and pour some of it into his mouth... There on the path near Sokil the collective farm horses have left droppings, nobody's planning on gathering them up."

That poor Maria... So, the way she was dressed in her Easter skirt, she lifted it up in the middle of the yard and pissed into the blue flame coming out of her son's mouth. His father and some visitor from outside the village held down Slavko, who had fallen onto the ground like a pig getting ready to be stuck.

Darusya started to feel bad for Slavko, who might burn up for nothing from the *horilka*,[7] and in the evening she brought him the last red apple from her cellar and gave it to Maria in silence. To which Maria's husband sighed: "People take *pysanky* to normal people,[8] but sweet Darusya brings her last apple to the roaring drunk.

Maria sat on the chair near the bed near Slavko's head, who was clearing his throat from beneath the quilted

---

6 According to village custom, married women should wear a scarf on their heads as a sign of their respectable status.

7 Ukrainian vodka. Its root word *hority* means "to burn."

8 The famous colorful Ukrainian Easter eggs with geometric patterns and symbols. The word for them comes from the verb "pysaty," which means to write. They are literally "written" in beeswax with a stylus before they are dipped in various dyes.

coat that had been thrown on him. And she was holding her head with both hands the same way that Darusya would hold it when she got an attack of pain, and she staggered back and forth exactly the same way, as though rusty rings were tearing her head.

And which of them now was stupid, Maria, her son, or both of them at the same time, Darusya truthfully didn't know.

That's why she goes to the river, sits on the bank right on the green grass that already reaches up toward the sun, and gazes at the water. Her head isn't hurting today. Today is Easter Sunday, and she put on really old shoes, but nevertheless her Easter best. And tomorrow Darusya will take them off till the next Easter Sunday and will walk barefoot until the river freezes over. And when it freezes over—she'll pull on her father's felt boots.

When she walks barefoot, the pain bothers her less. She sometimes even digs a hole in the middle of the garden to the height of her lower back, she lowers herself into it, wraps herself in the living black cover that tickles her body with broken roots, worms and rotted leaves, and she stands or sits in the living earth this way for hours. The earth takes away her pain and gives her the sap of life. It rises up along her body to her brow, as if along a tree trunk, and inside herself Darusya again feels strength that had been taken from her head by the red-hot iron of pain when it seemingly crawls out even through her ears and skin.

Then she thinks: is it good to make fun of her when at times she spends the day half buried in the earth while Tarasyk had been saved in the village this way when he was shocked by electricity? They buried him up to his neck, and the earth pulled death out of him. But no one made fun of Tarasyk's father, or his brothers who had placed him in the dug up hole as if it were a cemetery grave.

Why has the village made fun of unfortunate Darusya for years? Electricity struck Tarasyk *just one time*. But the pain strikes her head almost every day. What, should she wait for someone else's help? They can't even help themselves, why would they care about her? They should be happy for Darusya that she doesn't cause them problems. But heck... let them make the crazy sign with their hands. All the same, just stupid ones make it. If they would just stop reminding her about the candy.

*

People don't understand that Darusya saves herself any way she can. Sometimes with water, sometimes with earth, sometimes with herbs. Because more than anything she wants to live in this world, which is such a happy, colorful and fragrant one. When she is healthy she makes up for the lost time when she writhed in pain. She doesn't want to remember because she's already so wracked with pain that she doesn't know how she can walk on her legs.

But Darusya never complains about anything. She takes a faded little ball of colored wool threads, several scraps of wide tinsel folded in four, ribbons from the wedding wreath of Maria's daughter Anna, and she goes into her golden orchard, among the pear and apple trees planted by her father's hands. The apple trees already don't bear very good fruit. They're old. But the fruit still shines here and there among the sparse gold of the leaves. And the pear tree has completely dried up. It already has as many leaves as the hair on Pitryk's bald head.

Darusya shimmies up the pear tree and begins to tie tinsel strips around the sad branches. Why should the tree be sad, when the autumn sun warms up, when Darusya isn't wracked with pain in her brain? On Sunday Darusya always puts on her mother's embroidered blouse. And what, the pear tree can't have a blouse today, sewn by Darusya's hands? The tinsel shines in the sun, the wind rocks the colored threads on the red leaves—and Darusya wants to sing. But someone might hear. Singing also causes harm. Ivanna and Vasyl sang so much about a red guelder rose[9] that they carted them off to Siberia where they keep them to this very day. Or maybe they're not keeping them anymore, because there's nobody there anymore?!

Darusya hears and knows everything, she just doesn't speak to anyone. *They* think she's mute. But she's not. Darusya just doesn't *want* to speak. Words can cause harm. She doesn't know from where she remembers that, but it's the truth. After a little while—and Darusya remembers who told her that any kind of conversation can cause harm.

What of it if she doesn't speak? Mute Katrinka also just pantomimes, and no one calls her *stupid*. And Darusya hasn't swallowed her tongue, but all the same they tell

<hr />

9   A national emblem of Ukraine and the central image in a patriotic Ukrainian song. During Soviet times Ukrainians could be imprisoned for singing it.

lies about her. She's not sweet, but she's not stupid either. May God take them, the peoples' foolish tongues.

Darusya remembers how when she was still quite little, even before she learned about the taste of candies, how she and her neighbor Slavko twirled the crazy sign with their finger by their heads when stupid Paraska used to walk along the street. And the children, they thought she really was stupid, because that's what everyone in the village said because Paraska used to talk to herself out loud, she used to wave her arms and always used to threaten someone with a great big knobbly switch. For days at a time Paraska would walk among the houses, not asking for anything, not bothering anyone, with just the knobbly switch swaying in her arms like a village windmill, and Darusya asked her father how is it that Paraska's hands don't hurt from the switch, or her legs from walking?

Father took his birch switch, hidden in his house for such an occasion, and gave Darusya such a swat on her butt that for half a day she sat in the potato patch beyond the stable.

"Why did you beat me, father?" Darusya asked that evening after her eyes had dried from the tears, and her bottom had stopped burning. "Everyone says that Paraska's foolish. But Slavko and I didn't say it, we just gave the sign that she's weak in the head.

"Weak in the head—but they're God's people." That's all father said then.

"And what about us, aren't we all God's people?" Darusya asked in disappointment. "Momma sometimes is also weak in the head, but you, father, have never said that momma is one of God's people."

It may have been the first time father patted Darusya on her head:

"Darusya, sometimes our momma's head hurts because she fell down from the top of the dam. But she's not weak in the head. But Paraska's not all there. And that's why she's one of God's people, because only she can speak freely with God. But the rest of us aren't like Paraska. And may God grant that you, my sweet little child, never be the same kind of God's person as Paraska."

"So you, father, wouldn't want your Darusya to speak with God?"

"My sweet wonder…," father kissed Darusya on her brow. "Say an 'Our Father' and go to sleep. That's the best conversation you can have with God."

"Daddy, but when does the priest talk with God: when he says a prayer in church or when no one hears him?" Darusya refuses to back off.

Because of the priest she once got a good whupping from her father. And all because of Maria's Slavko. Only she and Slavko used to play together as children. Slavko always darted wildly through the garden like a mole, and even as a little girl Darusya was sedate, serious, like an old woman.

It often happened that Slavko incited her to do something foolish. That's how it happened that time. They were playing hide and seek in Maria's yard, amid several haystacks, a spacious woodcutting area, a barn, a root cellar dug out into a hill, an always pungent oil mill.

Some strange man in a green hat with a hatchet, leaning again the picket fence, for a long time followed the noisy running of Slavko and Darusya around the livestock pen until, finally, he addressed them respectfully. Darusya remembers how he beautifully and slowly took off his hat before them:

"Glory be to Jesus!"

"Glory to God forever!" They simultaneously answered the visitor from behind the picket fence.

"Who do you belong to, kids? To which *gazda*[10]?" The man took an interest.

"To different parents." Slavko answered. "I'm Maria's son, and she's Darusya. What did you want, pops?"

"Do you happen to know, kids, where the priest lives here?"

"The priest?" After thinking about it, Darusya asked. "Which one?"

"Why, do you have two priests?" The man began to laugh.

"Why do you need the priest?" Slavko leaned over the picket fence, and answered the question with a question.

"I want to baptize my child. I'm from the other side of the river, and we have one priest for three parishes. And yours, they say, is very good."

"Do you need the priest, the one with the beard, and in a cassock? The one who wears a tall black hat?" Slavko interrogated further.

"That's the one...."

"Then take tha-at road up there, and on that side, on a hill by the pear trees, that's where the priest lives."

---

10   *Gazda* and *gazdynya* are the typical polite forms of address, male and female respectively, for farm owners in the Carpathian Mountains. The word is actually Hungarian in origin with the same meaning. I have decided just to use the masculine form *gazda* throughout the translation to maintain local color instead of words such as "squire" or the more cumbersome "master/mistress of the farmstead."

"Slavko, the priest lives in the dell, past the church," Darusya tugged the neighbor boy by his sleeve, but the stranger with the hatchet already couldn't hear it since he disappeared beyond the stile on the other side of the street. "Vasyl lives near the plum trees."

*

...Darusya could still feel the way Daddy's belt danced on her skirt and along her legs that evening. Not only did the stranger feel ashamed after greeting Vasyl the carpenter with "Glory be to Jesus, God come to your aid, Father!," he nearly got a whipping himself. Because people in the village behind his back had nicknamed the carpenter "Father" for his Sunday dress, in which without fail he always went to church: a long coat, similar to a priest's robe, and a black hat. And after the guest, justifying himself, had explained from where they had sent him to the plum trees, Vasyl the carpenter didn't delay in coming to their house in the evening:

"Kind *gazda*, I know that you are a master, but I never would have thought you could teach your child so badly! You should be ashamed! Ashamed!" And spat at his feet.

Darusya to this day very well remembers daddy explaining to her afterward that not every person is the way people talk about them behind their back.

"People sometimes love to ridicule others, make up nicknames. And it doesn't always happen from spite. And it's not always the truth."

But is it insulting when you're called names?" Back then she wanted to know everything, as though someone had whispered to her or warned her about her own future.

"It's not insulting, child, if you're not a thief and not a liar...."

*

Darusya cries, having placed her uncovered head into a lonely red aster that had wandered among her deep blue and white sisters. The neighbor's pots clank on both sides of Darusya's household. You could tell Maria was cooking plum jam, because you could smell it all the way here, to the asters, and wasps hurled themselves in swarms from the wild plum trees to Maria's wooden smokehouse. And Vasyuta is pulling feathers—she's going to make pillows for her granddaughter, whose wedding is in the spring.

Maria always says beforehand:

"Darusya, I'll be making jam tomorrow."

And in the morning looks across the wicket fence: if Darusya walked around the garden, then she can place a fire into the wooden smoke house.

Maria is odd; she expects that Darusya doesn't understand why she tells her beforehand about the jam. But Darusya knows: Maria thinks that her jam is sweet. It's not sweet at all—it's tart, it bites her tongue and gums. And there's nothing in the world that's sweet except for candy. And Darusya doesn't want to talk about this even with Maria.

When Darusya thinks about candy just in her head when she is alone, her head never aches, but if someone just mentions it out loud—then her brain suffers like a dull hatchet: chop, chop, it gouges her bones, and it can't be cut off.

Let people eat candy as much as they want, just as long as Darusya doesn't have to hear about it. Then her head wouldn't hurt.

And Darusya eats Maria's jam in the winter. She takes bread or boiled corn meal, a bowl of jam, a cup of boiling water—and eats it for lunch, and even for dinner, and even in the middle of the night she could get up and scoop out a spoon or two. And when she eats, she always thinks: I would take daddy some jam, but for some reason he never asks for jam. But without a word from her father Darusya wouldn't dare. She knows *what he loves*.

Darusya cries because she hasn't been to her father's for a long time. She needed to cry herself out beforehand, because you couldn't in front of him. Maybe he's angry with her, but she's never gone to him empty-handed.

And she didn't go because she didn't have anything. There were no apples from spring. Last year's potatoes were gone, and this year's potato crop was bad, they were so small, like nuts in the forest. She'll give them to Maria's pigs. Pickled cabbage wasn't very good for father's digestion. It also wasn't fitting to bring him gruel without milk.

And the last time, two months had passed, or maybe even an entire three before she was able to churn a small fistful of butter from Maria's milk. Maria will bring a half-liter once every two or three days, and Darusya doesn't drink it—she leaves it to make sour cream. She collects it a few times—and the milk goes into the churning can and into the cellar. Again she waits for half a liter. And then from the sour milk she'll make some cheese. And only then will she go to father.

When she saw that there was entirely too little milk, because Maria's cow had started to kick, she went over to Pavlo's for a day to rake. The women waved their arms, took away the rakes, told the rakers to carry water from the washtub, and she didn't let the rake out of her hands till lunchtime when she heard a thin drill begin to drill through her head…. Just then did she put down her rake by the beech tree and went to the well. She poured and poured the chilled water on herself in buckets until there wasn't a dry thread on her, and the drills grew quiet.

Pavlo's wife then gave her a little sheep's milk cheese, a small handful of cheese, and a bucket of potatoes. There would be enough of those goods for an entire wedding.

*

Darusya always got ready to go to father's starting in the early morning.

She washed up for a long time.

She combed her hair even longer.

She put her braid up in a crown.

She tied it up with two scarves: a white one and a black one.

She dressed warmly. On top of her fur-trimmed wool jacket she threw half a well-worn, long ago faded wool blanket.

And that's how she sat on the bench nearly the entire day.

"Sweet Darusya has gotten ready to go see her father," she heard someone's voice from the street and didn't even want to recognize it.

"You can see she's hidden away some milk, the orphan," another, also unrecognizable voice answered.

When Darusya was getting ready to visit her father, she understood very little. No, it's wrong to put it this way—she did understand, but she showed no sign of it. Once she didn't even recognize Maria when she placed a small bowl with several eggs on the bench near her.

Why should she recognize Maria when Darusya was not taking eggs to her father? He refuses even to look at eggs from the time when at Easter he got heartburn right after gobbling up five Easter eggs at one sitting.

Darusya sits by the house and collects her thoughts. She has to put all she needs to say to her father in order in her head. Darusya tells him everything, asks him about everything, but for the longest time listens to her father's slow, hard-to-hear conversation. Only she never cries in front of him. Darusya's father doesn't *like* Darusya crying. And she doesn't want to rile him.

When the sun falls low but still hasn't set, Darusya takes her Easter basket, spreads out over the bottom half of a cloth embroidered with the image of the Mother of God, places cheese there wrapped in cheesecloth, butter, a liter-sized can of milk, a little, but not a lot, of bread, a scrap of sandpaper, she covers it all with the other half of the cloth, takes the basket onto her arm, latches the gate closed, and steps out into the middle of the street.

Darusya walks to her father only along the middle of the street, cars are moving, carts, people go slowly— Darusya doesn't care: on the road to her father she is a *princess.* When young people rush to get to their wedding, or a corpse is being carried to the graveyard—they don't yield from the middle of the road, and no one contradicts that custom. Why shouldn't Darusya be allowed to do the same?

She once even asked her father why each young wife walks to her wedding this way, as though the entire street were hers and hers alone.

"Because before her wedding she—is a princess," her father answered.

"And after the wedding?" Darusya asked.

For some reason father sighed: "An unhappy woman."

Until Darusya becomes unhappy, she always will walk to him like a princess. And no one will tell her otherwise.

It's true it happens rarely that Darusya walks through the village like a princess. Though she's not lazy, she tries not to be a nuisance. Let father rather ask her why she hasn't visited him in such a long time than make a face, thinking that his daughter is walking like a horse cart without a hitch.

Darusya walks along the middle of the road—and next to her like maids of honor the village dogs, whose owners don't keep them chained to their dog houses, tremble in a dignified way. By the time she makes her way to her father, she'll gather about two-dozen of them. They walk—they don't bark, but just wag their tails, like small peeled off Hutsul wedding saplings;[11] they stick out their tongues, and show their white teeth.

11   The Hutsuls in the Carpathians symbolically use a sapling during the traditional wedding ceremony. It is described here in detail (in Ukrainian): http://www.wz.lviv.ua/articles/85302. Thanks to Olha Tytarenko for providing the reference.

But this is a time when no one can placate Darusya—not even the dogs. For her to toss them a bit of boiled corn meal—God forbid, her hands would dry up and her legs removed if she, a princess, would think about anyone other than her father. And so they walk—taking up the entire street, from ditch to ditch, and though the music isn't playing, they're somehow walking along cheerfully, lively, you feel like looking at them sometimes more than at a group of people.

Sweet Darusya always glides along in the company of the dogs along the desolate village street, and sometimes several motors snort behind them, but don't dare to pass by this strange procession, the way that knowing drivers don't pass either funerals or weddings.

They already reach the club. In order to see her father, near the club you have to turn *past Yorchykha*, as they say in the village. In this here house to the right of the current village club there once lived a woman. Either from Austria or from Romania. Her name was Yorchykha, because her husband's name was Yorko. Few people remember when the Yorkos kicked the bucket, or if someone helped them meet their maker. A long time ago strangers built great mansions on the spot of the Yorkos' house, gave birth and schooled little children, and were lords of their property as only they knew how, and that's how the place in the village that no one could avoid was stamped in memory: right *past Yorchykha's....*

"*You, Odokiyka, why are you buying these embroidered cloths[12]?*"

---

12   Embroidery plays a significant role in traditional Ukrainian folk customs and is used in virtually all religious rites including Baptism, marriage, and burial. The embroidered *rushnyk* or embroidered cloth represents a protection from evil.

"What do you mean why? I'm going past Yorchykha's place."

"It's still too early for you, God forbid!"

"It's never too early to think about tomorrow. You need to fear God for another thing, and not for that. So I advise you: buy the embroidered cloths while you are still alive, because they might be gone…."

"Listen, Maruska, what's happenin' with our people in this here world, where's you don't sees harmony from nowhere, and you can't sees no end to their stupidity."

"Dearie, let people go past Yorchykha's more often— from there you can see everything so well, no, really, a lot better than from Chornohora."[13]

But people don't usually rush to go past Yorchykha's for no reason. Maybe they also don't have anything to go with, the way Darusya didn't. Maybe they don't have the time. But Darusya already has the time.

Near the club she takes a sharp left turn, crosses a wide little wooden bridge and finally stands in front of the gate. The gate is always locked here with a little wooden stick. Darusya places her basket on the ground, pulls out the stick, pokes it into the ground, opens half the gate, and then looks around. The dogs, lowering their snouts, stand in a semicircle around Darusya, as though they're guarding her. She looks for a long time at them, pets each one on their head, she leans forward as if she's giving them orders, takes the basket into her hand, and steps past the gate.

The comforted dogs sit down in a tight circle by the open gate, vigilantly gazing in every direction until

13   Chornohora literally means "black mountain." It is the tallest mountain range in the Ukrainian Carpathians.

Darusya disappears among the trees and flowers. The dogs not only wait for Darusya here, even when she would return from her father in the dark, but they also give the sign to all others: when Darusya is beyond the gate, we don't recommend you go there.

More than one soul has taken heels to the fields when the dogs are on guard near Yorchykha's.

*

The low gates next to her father's little house are closed, and Darusya enters quietly, as though she's afraid to startle the owner. Just as last time, she can't see her father. She just hears his voice. It's as though it's emanating from under the ground—and makes its way so quietly, barely audibly, that she immediately sits on the ground onto the tall uncut grass right next to her father's threshold where bustling ants immediately attack her. She feels so strange, wondrous, even sweet. Yes. She senses either sweetness, or faintness in her chest—but oh wonder!—from that sweetness her head also becomes better.

To Darusya it seems that her poor soul has left her for a certain amount of time and has flown toward father's voice. There was left just one body, as though it's not Darusya's, not in pain, and not blackened, but someone else's, cold, unknown body, along which ants happily crawl. She sits, stock still, almost not breathing, with eyes shut, as though she's afraid that here-here her soul will return to her body, but no longer with her father's voice.

And the voice floats from everywhere, like the setting sun, tender, unreproachful, patient. And Darusya bends her now so clear obedient head, without knowing herself before whom: either before the sweet sun, or this voice that envelops her from her feet to her head, as though it wants to warm her, or give her love, or to pity her....

Finally, caressed with her father's slowly disappearing voice, with her soul returned to her body, Darusya lazily opens her eyes, rises up from the ground, and only then looks all around.

She hasn't been here for so long! How shamelessly she let father's farmstead fall into neglect! Broken by the wind, yellowing strands of thick grass nod their tiny heads: long ago, oh so long ago, daughter....

Darusya tears off the faded grass, carries it off beyond the gate of the iron fence with traces of fairly recent paint, or even more—rust. She takes the sandpaper, cleans off the reddish crust, and wipes the iron rods with a cloth. Then she goes to where her father's head is in the grave. She rests against the top of the cross—and again stands for a long time, grows still, and from time-to-time just nods her head, as though in a sign of agreement with the voice heard and understood by only her. She spreads her arms apart, embraces the cross, and again for a long time clings to it.

Then she blows away dust from the cross, wipes it with the cloth, tugs all four columns of the enclosure in turn and finally sits down at the feet of the grave, which settled long ago and was nearly the same height as the earth around it.

Darusya slowly places her ear to the earth—but in a moment she suddenly leaps up. She fussily searches all around, then strikes her brow with her hand, removes from her shoulders the worn half of the woolen blanket and with it covers the lower part of the grave, as though covering her father's frozen feet. Can he, so frozen, so overworked at his age, really keep warm with just the grass or the soil?

When Darusya goes up to her waist in the water or stands in a hole dug up to her lower back—she's not seeking warmth, she's seeking relief for her head. She steps into the water or into the earth not for very long—just until the fire leaves her forehead. But if she had lain down in the cold earth for years, like her father, she'd have to find warmth.

Here her father's voice just said that he's so cold, that she'll warm him up a bit. This way she strokes his gaunt chest through the cold clay, carefully touches his fingers, combs his hair. And then she'll feast. For even the church filled with the most people in the village is not as joyful as Darusya's feasting here with her father.

It's good she has *something* she can treat him to today! Darusya takes the stored goods out of her basket and lays them around the cross, unwraps the cheese from the cheesecloth, then butter, pinches off a bit of cheese, and tosses it in her mouth. She chews it for a long time. And then she bends close to the cross and it's as if she's whispering something into its black upper part, as though into someone's ear. Her lips move so expressively that if you were to lean over to her, you could clearly hear words.

Darusya whispers for a long time, hotly, fervently, just from time to time tears herself away from the cross, looking all around, scans everything all around her with her eyes, and again falls to the ground, and whispers quickly, as though she's afraid that someone will hear her dreadful language.

She never lights a candle here. Because a candle burns and burns and burns out everything human all around. The fire of the candle chases away not only an evil spirit, but also the spirit of a person, who wasn't always dead. And when the spirit disappears—then you mourn for the dead person less and less, until you stop mourning completely.

That is why Darusya doesn't like people who light candles at graves. They want more quickly to rid themselves of their pain that breathes from beneath the sad grave's clay. People run away from sorrow that enters the soul in stinging pain just as their eyes catch sight of the cross. People don't like to grieve. In general they don't like anything.

And Darusya doesn't want not to grieve for her father. Because for her here it's not grief—here, near her father—as much as there is so much real life here. Everything bad has passed, turned pale, lost its clarity, and grief for something far away remained so sharp in Darusya's head, that it hurts her from it. And if her father doesn't console her—then no one will help Darusya. That is why she doesn't burn the candle: she's afraid that she'll come here some time—and the voice that always floats from here, like the sun, that you don't know where it comes from, will no longer meet her. What would she do then?

There are no more potatoes, just a handful of flour remains, for a long time she hasn't had anything in order to churn butter for her father. You can endure everything. Even the long time not coming to the grave. Everything. But each time Darusya approaches the grave, her soul also curls up like a snail from fear that right then dead silence—without her father's voice—will meet her. If his voice is gone—she will be gone too. Without his voice why should she go on living?

No one, not a single soul in the world knows that Darusya's lips become unbound here. Sometimes she thinks that she herself doesn't know about this.

When she first tried to speak with father, she got terribly frightened of her own voice. Then it seemed to her that the entire world had heard it, and even worse—the entire village, it was so sonorous and loud. Darusya knew for sure that she said just one word: "Daddy…," and the voice itself moved from her throat, as though it had never disappeared, and produced certain strange wonders, it teased, it played, it spread about, scooted off between the trees and the graves, and returned again, silver, to her— she so wanted to catch it with her hands to hide it in her bosom, or in her pockets, or anywhere else from which she'd be able to take it, but in such as way that no one in the world would know.

Frightened, she looked around for a long time as though she were searching for the true owner of the voice, she walked between the neighboring crypts, looked under the slabs, felt the trees. A certain silence reigned at the graveyard, just her "daddy" continued to resonate in the crowns of trees, in the grass, in her throat. And she repeated: "Daddy…"—quietly, with just her lips, chasing the sounds into her throat, into the deepest corner of her being. And then she heard her father's answer. So close, next to her, as though he were sitting here, near her, and she heard his warmth.

She never knew how to be joyous, but at that time a certain force raised Darusya to her feet and she whirled between the graves, the tilted crosses, her skirt *twirling in the air....*

"*...Do you hear, Marika, for years I never said this to anyone, but I'll tell you now, because they can take me away past Yorchykha's, then I'll remain with a sin.... This somehows was a few years ago. I'm a carrying milk to the daughter-in-law, that piece of dog bone, may lightning strike her, when she was so neglectful taking care of her child, she should never have any children ever.... I goes along the cemetery, and it's getting dark, and from birth I've always been afraid of cemeteries, I goes really briskly, I looks down at my feet and says an Our Father just in case. Then I hear—from Dovbush's grave, and you know, he's right at the very corner, right by the road, an unclean force is speaking, speaking in a human voice, and so terrifying, and so coarse, like a bear ripping through raspberry bushes.*

Listen, good woman, I, as I was walking, so I tumbled down the path, my strength left me, I couldn't either stand, or scream... and that's not all... And in between the graves, so's I'd be healthy, a specter in human form dances. God help me, it was as though it's dancing the "The Hutsul Girl" at a wedding, swirling, holding its hands wide apart, so its skirt rises up high. And the voice, merciful God, like it had torn out of the cellar. And always saying "daddy," "daddy"... I already thought that my mind was leaving me forever, then I started to bow in prayer, and cross myself, and cross my-

self… And here from the cemetery gate sweet Darusya steps out and she's somehow wondrous and strange, and so similar to that specter, that I, I'm tellin' the truth, Maria, I couldn't count to two or three: who of us is stupid, and who is smart. If I didn't know she doesn't know how to speak, I'd take a sin upon myself against her, Maria… may God forgive my sin."

"And it's all from the fact, dear Varvara, that you didn't confess this year…. and you're sinning against your daughter-in-law… That's God sending you signs."

"Ayay-ay, Maria… that's true—I didn't confess when I had to confess, it happened like that…."

"If sweet Darusya begins to speak it will be when she's past Yorchykha's. It's a sin to commit a sin against a cripple, my silver Varvara…."

*

…With such effort she hid that she knew how to speak that at times she herself didn't believe otherwise. She locked the doors, curtained the windows, with two fingers pulled out her tongue, took the mirror and kept looking, as though she were waiting, for the words to walk out of her throat by themselves. Her tongue was long and red. Darusya tugged it here and there—not a sound. Once in the middle of the night she tried to speak. She pinched herself. Her skin hurt. She was left with a bruise. But her speech didn't return to her. She couldn't even bawl like an infant. Then with her weak head she understood that her speech would return to her only when she would go to see her father.

And she was afraid of going to her father often. What if someone suddenly follows her?! They'll tattle on her that she's not mute, and not stupid, and not sweet?! For Darusya this is more terrifying than the attacks of pain. Let her stupid noggin hurt and crack, but it won't return her speech for anything. She can't live among people with *her language*. People themselves have taught her not to speak. So let them tolerate her muteness. Doesn't she tolerate their idiocy?

And here in the cemetery father understood Darusya and kept telling her. How to live, how to endure, not to hold a grudge, not to be embarrassed in front of people, to forgive intentional and unintentional evil. Here she understood everything. Nearly just about everything, to the smallest little thing. She'd return home—and everything would fly away, like a dried up pine cone, and great black sorrow would again creep into her head. And then she would have doubts: maybe she really was stupid. Not sweet, just stupid?...

But just as she would return home, father would come to her dreams and torment Darusya out of her mind. The entire night he would stand at the door, not crossing the threshold, black, unshaven, ragged, with an outstretched hand asking for milk. She wanted to say that all the milk, all the sour cream, and cheese, and butter that she had hidden away for months, she gave him yesterday—but her tongue was mute. Just her arms flailed like crows above the bed in despair, so that by morning she didn't understand who had made such a mess of her bed.

Broken, with swollen eyes, Darusya ran from house to house in the morning, she carried an empty cup with traces of milk on the bottom, showing it to the mistresses of the farmsteads.

"It's begun…," Maria, to whom Darusya always came first, crossed herself silently.

"You should have used your head…," Slavko, when he was home, would babble. But when he was home—he was always drunk.

"Shut up, may lightning strike you! Don't you see, she's walking barely alive…."

*

She heard everything and understood it all. But how can she say that she's not guilty? What, call them all to the cemetery and tell them?! And Darusya knows: besides to her father, she'll never speak to anyone again in this life. And won't even make a confession before she's ready to go past Yorchykha's.

…She was carrying milk, clotted milk, sour cream, cheese—everything poured and shaken up into a single three-liter can—she placed it near the cross and indescribably was astonished: from her yesterday's victuals there really was little remaining. Father did remain hungry after all.

When in the middle of the night her father's outstretched hand awakened her, she knew that in a day or two her head would begin to ache. She took clean scarves, a can of badger lard, a match, and a candle—and placed them on a bench near her bed. She also walked all around the garden, and trimmed the grass for her only chicken, and already felt the thin, stinging leeches getting drunk on her forehead as though they were drilling it. And each time she thought that perhaps this is it, *her time had come*….

In the morning Maria would find Darusya with her head covered with five scarves, turned toward the wall, with a pallid face, about which it was difficult to say whether it was the face of a corpse, or a living person....

IVAN TSVYCHOK
THE PREVIOUS DRAMA

"Marika, I'll tell you one thing: if you're not happy in childhood…."

"What are you talking about, Varvarka?"

"About what… About who! About sweet Darusya and Ivan Tsvychok. Just look at those two unfortunate people," she nods across the picket fence into the neighboring yard. "May God spare you from such misfortune… They've leaned their heads to one another and don't say a word, and don't pay attention to normal people…."

"Who knows, dear Varvarka, what they are now: happy or unhappy… who knows… Maybe there's something to it that they're sitting like this way—and the whole world doesn't concern them…."

"Have you gone nuts, Maria, sayin' such a thing?! Will a normal person sit around this way in broad daylight and listen to a fool play the drymba[14]?"

"Maybe I've gone nuts. Who knows when a person goes nuts… But mull it over in your mind—and try to remember the last time you sat with your man leaning head to head while he was playing a drymba for you instead of playing on your nerves?!"

"You're asking such nonsense!.. A man of the house isn't about playing a drymba for his wife."

"It depends, dear Varvarka…."

"I see, Maria, around these two you have somehow become dazed too. It's not surprising given the neighbors…."

---

14 The *drymba* is an onomatopoetic word in Ukrainian for what in English is called a jaws harp or a Jew's harp. I've decided to keep the Ukrainian word in the text to convey the onomatopoetic sound and the nearly exalted nature of the instrument for the Hutsul people in the Carpathians.

…Ivan Tsvychok moved in with sweet Darusya—he was a strange and foolish man—as they thought in the village—a newcomer.

No one in Cheremoshne knew for sure when and where Ivan had his umbilical cord chopped off, where he was baptized, who his mother and father were, and whether he at least had a farmstead, or either a house or home. It seemed like he was simultaneously always and everywhere.

Few people hear Tsvychok speak, but when he says something… it's better not to bother him. It's better to listen to his *drymba* and think about something of your own that you wouldn't say out loud.

The bus is going to Vyzhnytsia: Ivan is sitting in the back seat right at the window—playing his *drymba*. Some of the passengers, maybe, would argue with their neighbor for an impolite movement or accidental jostling—but will look at Ivan, shrug their shoulders, and bite their tongues.

And Ivan looks through the window, quickly fingers near his lips—and extracts such a melody from his *drymba* that it slowly grows quiet in the bus as if in the presence of a corpse. Just the driver shouts from the front: "I'd pay you myself, Ivan, just to ride with me every day and calm down people, because if you listen your fill of that one fine day, you don't want to live. So I listen to the *drymba*—and I'm happy, as though I'm going to my mother's."

That same day the bus was making its way to Kosiv—and Ivan was already there as usual. He leans his back on the rear door of the bus—and doesn't stop playing the *drymba*. All kinds of people are on board: one is as happy as a cemetery at midnight. But when he listens to Ivan, he doesn't say anything, because he thinks Tsvychok is dumb, but Ivan can blurt out something that would make you jump off the bus in the middle of the road. One day he so vilified a young woman from Tiudiv that the poor girl walks on foot to Kuty so as not to run into Tsvychok.

And it was like this. Ivan was playing away on his *drymba* in the bus, and a young woman says something smart-alecky to him; most likely, she asked if it wasn't cold for him to sleep at bus stations.

Ivan kept silent.

But the girl makes fun of him further, and also looks around if the menfolk are listening to her.

Ivan put the *drymba* into his pocket, wiped his lips, and so the whole bus could hear, asked, as though he had started to shoot a machine gun:

"Didn't you, wicked wench and nasty slut, get any calluses on your wrinkly thing after the wedding in Rizhnya that week when you sent your legs flying up in the air while rolling in the hay with that *tsymbaly*[15] player until the silver fir trees — let alone people — covered their eyes in shame?"

Then he took the *drymba* to his lips again.

...No one knew or ever asked about Ivan's last name. From the time of the beginning of the world and sun, people and children in Cheremoshne nicknamed him Tsvychok, because from the villages surrounding the railway Ivan loved to collect "tsvyakhy" (nails), locally

15   A stringed instrument in the Carpathians similar to a hammer dulcimer.

called "tsvyky," from which he would then make *drymbas* and sell them either in Kuty or in Kosiv at the flea market.

The *drymbas* weren't just an instrument for playing, but also nearly the only form of income for Ivan, and Tsvychok nearly the only master craftsman of the *drymba* in all the surrounding mountains.

You wouldn't say that even here in the mountains there were a lot of *drymba* lovers, because this was not a time for merriment: it was rarer to hear the local trio music, and more often—the *trembita*.[16] But Ivan's *drymbas* were in demand, and even more often than the *drymbas* of those solitary makers who still were bold enough to compete with Tsvychok's work.

Tsvychok's instruments were bought for schools and village clubs, where on Sundays so-called ensembles of *drymba* players gathered and played on their *drymbas* like on *tsymbaly*.

The local exotic charm—the clothing, *pysanky*, songs and dances—from time to time was taken to the *oblast*[17] center for television, to festivals, or just to put on a show for the authorities.

So all the same the need for *drymbas*—though it wasn't considerable—always existed.

But no one, not even the biggest performer, can play the *drymba* as tastily as just about the way any buxom Hutsul girl can from her own secret knowledge and obvious experience.

16   A long horn used for long distance communication in the Carpathian Mountains by the Hutsuls.

17   An "oblast" is a governed area roughly the size of a state, and a "raion" roughly the equivalent to a county. I've translated "raion" here as "district."

A Hutsul girl sits herself down in the grass flooded by the sun on a hill or somewhere underneath a silver fir—and the world doesn't trouble her: she fingers the *drymba*, and she doesn't need Buckingham Palace, or a husband, or a lover on the side, or firewater.

White sheep graze in the grassy blanket and ring their bells as though they're giving a sign from paradise itself.

Hawks silver from the sun hang above her head.

A light wind sways the tiny heads of the grass.

Total silence hangs above the mountains and valleys.

And you feel like either dying or singing.

It's beautiful.

Some young women love the *drymba* more than the spinning wheel. They direct their eyes at Tsvychok's bag more ardently than at their husband's pants; they wait until Ivan sets out the new *drymbas* somewhere at the bus stations or right under the wooden fence.

True, some of the young women are somewhat embarrassed to express openly their desire for a *drymba*, so at first they ask Ivan about new knives or files, but their eyes always seek out among the metal merchandise a *drymba*, the body of which recalls that of a stout woman.

Who knows... maybe in the *drymba* women truly recognized themselves: indifferent and listless until the moment you take them in your hands, and when you take them, you'll hear such juicy warbling and delicate wails, that your heart becomes overwhelmed with tears and song at the same time, and you won't understand where the night is, or where the sun is, because only a woman's body so sumptuously quivers from a caress, like the body of the *drymba* from fingers....

41

And so the young village wives bought—some secretly, some openly—Tsvychok's *drymbas*; they nearly kissed his hands out of delight because they had a plaything that reminded them of themselves....

And the fact that they made fun of Ivan Tsvychok wasn't very odd: in this land they made fun of everyone.

"Petro, did you somewheres buy them kind of pants for church for folks? Or you imitatin' Tsvychok's style?"

"Do you hear, Ivanykha, why do you look like Tsvychok fooled around with you that night?"

...Ivan talked little about everything in this world besides the *drymba* and iron, with which he spoke both with his tongue and with his hands. He also had a birth defect: his tongue adhered to his palate—and as a result of that, his speech reminded you of the rattling of a car on a village street... Maybe that's why he didn't like to talk in public. Or maybe, he didn't really like people much, but just liked working for them. Who knows?

He lived where he could: he spent the night at bus stations, in church bell towers, in haysheds in the summer. Some of the village men sometimes hired Ivan to cut grass or to chop firewood, but he didn't have a great inclination to work on someone else's farmstead. That is why approximately the same conversation always occurred between a village employer and Tsvychok:

"Ivan, would you maybe come over on Monday for some mowing? The grass has been standing too long, and it's hard to find someone to mow it."

"On Monday?" Tsvychok asked again lazily. "Monday, kind *gazda*, is a difficult day. Either in winter or in summer. So Monday won't work. It's not a problem for the grass till it dies."

"Then my dear Ivan, come over on Tuesday."

"Eh-h-h, no, Tuesday's a troublesome day. I can't go on the road on Tuesday. And mowin'—that's also goin' on the road."

"And how about Wednesday?"

"Wednesday's a day of fasting.[18] And I love fish. You might not have fish. And if you do, then it's not the kind I need. So don't rush to mow on Wednesday. Or mow without me.

"Ivan, will you come on Thursday?"

"On Thursday, definitely not. On Thursday I have to shave. That's also a big job. And there, you see, it's already Friday. And on Friday they've called me to Petrashi to a wedding to prepare the groom for the ceremony. On Saturday I have a visit with a young woman. And getting ready for that takes a long time. So, I be sorry. Maybe come over to hire me for mowin' next week. But not Monday, 'cause Monday's a hard day...."

Take notice, one who happened to be a witness of such a long conversation with Ivan Tsvychok should be considered a happy person. Because everyone else couldn't boast of hearing more than two or three words from him.

On rare occasions Ivan agreed to live at some young woman's place. If he did, it wasn't for very long, and he wouldn't live with anyone else in the same village. And no young girl managed to keep him for more than two months. If Ivan cleaned out the main house or porch and laid out a wet floor cloth in front of the threshold, that meant he was thanking that house and that woman of

18   Fasting in the Ukrainian church (eating no meat or dairy products) occurs on certain church holidays, on Fridays, and during the Lenten season.

the house, and was going to wander off where his eyes would take him.

Because of this very few had any desire to take in Tsvychok to live with them. To sleep over for the night, if you please, but not more. And to tell the truth, the young women of the village, those who were really noble, or considered themselves that way, felt aversion for that unsuccessful, untidy man, that, in human language, represented a not very quick-witted, ill-fated, and unlucky man. And a woman determined to interrupt her orphaned fate through Ivan, or to taste the sweets with a man, even though it was with a dim guy, all the same—was rewarded with mocking jeers from the more fortunate and happy women for a long time.

"Vasylynka, you look as if you've been rolling around with Ivan for two nights…."

"I think, Parasochka dear, that just one night would be enough for you to have such a look, because you wouldn't be able to stand two nights next to Ivan, even if he'd want you… but, you see, he doesn't… you're not to his taste, for sure. So all that's left for you is to think about how Tsvychok rolls me around in the middle of the night…."

"And haven't you heard, dear Hafiyka, that it's true that Yilena got big with seed that night with Tsvychok?"

"Well, not everyone, Varvarka, goes to communion only in church. From time to time—you can taste a sinful body. But why would you care about Yilena when she's been a widow for five years?! And people say you aren't a widow, and you're in church taking communion, but you don't steer clear of sinning with other men."

"Since you're asking me this, then I'll tell you the truth: my grandmother gave me this desire for sin like a wedding

dowry. You're still young, so you don't know. But I know from my mother that our grandmother had seven children—and all of them from different fathers."

"Well, then why does the thought about Ivan torment you so much? Or do you want to try him out and just can't say it?"

*

...Once in the spring Ivan Tsvychok was chopping wood at Maria's, Darusya's nearest neighbor. How Maria convinced Tsvychok to go to work on her farmstead— God only knows. But facts are facts. Nearly the entire village looked and wondered how Ivan, taking off his checkered shirt, was able to wield his ax for nearly half a day—like a house on fire, and Maria was inexpressibly pleased.

You already know: no one can say that Ivan was such a good worker, because in the middle of working he could sit down on a stump or on a bench near the wall and either play the *drymba*, or gather up his clothes and start off toward the bus station.

He did almost the same at Maria's. He all of a sudden threw his ax into the middle of the yard, and so—since he was bare to his waist—leaned up against the wooden fence, pulled out his *drymba* from his pants—and played in the direction of Darusya's yard some very sorrowful melody, so sorrowful that the chickens stopped rummaging in the dust, and the dog began to wag his tail and set off for the doghouse.

In the meantime, Darusya, tied in wedding ribbons, bareheaded, with a wreath on her head, in a long white embroidered shirt, all the way to her heels, slit halfway, sat in the dried out pear tree tying up the branches, taking off the ribbons from her hair one by one. One moment she lifted her gaze to the sky, the next moment— she stared into her hands—and a solitary tear rolled along her cheek as though along a dried out ditch.

And Tsvychok played his *drymba* and looked across the wooden fence, as though not at Darusya, but just at her yard, then suddenly stuffed the *drymba* into his pants, put on his shirt, took his ax, silently opened up the gate to Darusya's farmstead, and started to chop her wood that had been carelessly tossed near the wall of her shed perforated with holes on every side.

Darusya kept looking at Ivan from the pear tree. She wiped her tears and slowly crawled off the tree, leaving the wreath from her head on a branch.

While she carried the wood into the shed and tidily stacked it by the wall, then gathered the chips and stacked them separately, then swept the yard, in the meantime Ivan again began playing the *drymba*, repeating to himself under his breath:

"Damn those dumb people, who from a smart person make a dumb one," and spat from time to time at his feet.

After all this Darusya opened the door for Ivan to her entryway.

Tsvychok entered her house in the same way in silence.

Maria just shrugged her shoulders in her yard: sweet Darusya doesn't open the door of her house by herself for anyone.

...From that day Ivan Tsvychok moved into Darusya's house.

Most often the days in their yard passed approximately this way: Ivan fashions a *drymba*—and Darusya, with a braid arranged nicely around her head, looks out from the shed, crossing her arms over her chest. And so in a somewhat domestic way, warmly, with a barely smiling face, she stands stationary and devours his work with her eyes.

Tsvychok silently keeps making the *drymbas*—and takes a bag filled with them somewhere out into the world for a week. And then from Storonets to Vyzhnytsia, from Vyzhnytsia to Kuty and Verkhovyna, in the passenger compartments of buses, the *drymba* quivers in his lips like a virgin just before sinning, and he extracts from it first humorous, then compassionate melodies— so that one day a certain young woman from Roztoky with packs and buckets of cherries rode all the way to Yablunytsia, missing her stop at Roztoky because she had become enamored of Tsvychok's playing.

The days of selling passed—and as strange as it was, from spring to fall Ivan returned to Darusya's yard and took to working first with his ax: to fix the wooden fence, to put the gate in order, to chop wood—and there again made his *drymbas*.

And it happened, in the middle of making *drymbas*, he simply sits down in the middle of the yard and takes a *drymba* to his lips. And after that there's no work going on either in this or in the neighbor Maria's livestock pen, because the two women are sitting on two opposite sides of the fence—each thinking her own thoughts, if she is still able to think, and Tsvychok extracts such sorrow from the body of the *drymba* that your heart would break even if it were made of stone.

...A heart is a heart, but when Darusya heard the voice of Ivan's *drymba*, her head never ached.

Then she would walk around the edge of the garden, or listen to the simple emotive melody, bowing her head to her knees, or would sit with Maria by the wall on a bench—and the iron rings pressing on her head fell from her like leaves from a tree, and it somehow became so easy—she didn't even feel like opening her eyes in the morning, and just wanted to lie that way—on the bed or in a sunny spot—and be happy that the pain had disappeared, as if she had never had it.

And maybe only Maria knew that Darusya's head doesn't ache, and that she's not running to the water, and not digging holes for herself in the earth, and not climbing up the pear tree when Ivan takes to playing his *drymba*. So Maria was willing to carry crocks of borsht or mashed beans, a little thick gruel, or a piece of pig lard to her neighbors every day so that Ivan would just not be hungry, so that he had the strength to play the *drymba*. Because Tsvychok's ribs shone through his shirt—no one knows if his family was that gaunt, or whether a restless life had so dried out the man.

And Ivan oftentimes returns Maria's meals, pointing to a pot of cooked potatoes or a cast iron pot of thick gruel, and adds calling after her:

"You think you're a *gazda*, and I don't disagree, but my arms don't grow out of my ass, Maria."

So when Ivan was in the village, nearly every day he sat down with his *drymba* on the threshold with Darusya near him. And just like that the day passed for them.

And then a few days passed—Ivan again made his *drymbas* or set off into the wide world with them, and Darusya fell in the house on her bed—and for entire days at a time looked at the ceiling, not raising herself up either to her food or to the stove, not even to a lonesome chicken that was pecking right at the windows...."

"Birds of a feather flock together," the young women in the village, lovers of lies and scandals, shrugged their shoulders. On the other hand no scandals ever left Darusya's yard, unless Ivan got out of hand on buses as never before. It was frightening to offend him, because he might utter something from which you'd need to flee the village.

*

...A strange thing, but one time sweet Darusya took Tsvychok to the cemetery to her father. As always, she got ready in the late afternoon, put together a basket, and, in front of Ivan, opened the gate to the street.

Ivan thought about it for a while—and then went back to the house.

Disheartened Darusya stood there, with one hand holding on to the wooden fence, and with the other the basket, staring at the door to the house.

Ivan came out in a summer hat that was a tight fit for his head, holding a scythe behind his back.

This is the way they toddled along: Darusya with her basket in front, Ivan Tsvychok with the scythe tossed over his shoulder a half a step behind her, and all around them—the village dogs, who weren't driven by their masters into their dog houses and who weren't tied to their chains.

Behind them cars chugged,
a cart rattled,
two boys pedaled their bicycles –
and no one dared to pass the odd and slow procession until it turned past Yorchykha's beyond the club.

While Darusya went to her father, Ivan stood at the gate with the dogs, and just as Darusya showed herself before them, Ivan went deep into the cemetery.

The next morning Maria said that Ivan cut nearly half the cemetery's grass and weeds, and especially those graves that no one tended.

But after that Ivan somehow became so ferocious and spiteful—he said very little even to Darusya.

…At a certain time Tsvychok returned after his usual travels, with scraps of iron pipes hanging on him in such a way that his head barely peeped out from behind all of them.

And by morning a forge had practically been made in Darusya's yard: Ivan makes-fixes-cleans-sands the pipes, and sniffles his nose, but no one hears him, and no one gets in the way. Only Maria casts fearful glances over the wooden fence from time to time, but she keeps silent, poor woman, in order not to run into Tsvychok's vicious tongue.

And after the midday meal, the children ran to Darusya's yard quicker than to school. And all of them with iron rods, and pipes, and nuts, and washers. The children carry iron as though they were taking it to a transfer station, and Tsvychok barks out orders loudly: short pieces of iron—by the wall, long pipes—into the house, nuts and nails—into the wicker basket.

After the end of the project, Ivan sat the boys on a bench by the house, grabbed a water bucket, and went to the center of the village to a store, brought back seven-kopeck biscuits from there, giving one to each child, and presented each with a *drymba*, and finally sent them off on their way home.

Darusya looked at all this from her window through the curtain, leaning her brow to the pane and closing her mouth with her hand. That is how Ivan found her as he came into the house to get a drink of water.

And in the morning—in the wee hours—such a loud moaning and groaning kicked up in Darusya's yard as if someone had been stabbed to death or their fingers had been caught in a door.

The nearby neighbors ran to the shouts and found the following picture: sleepy Darusya, wrapped in several scarves. She was leaning out through the window nearly to her bellybutton in a white nightshirt; and Ivan, in just his drawers, flew out like a bullet from the cattle shed. He wasn't able to clean off the hay from his head that, evidently, had served as a pillow for him. And in the middle of the yard the wife of the collective farm brigade leader Perederiy—Iryna—was loudly moaning and groaning, and somehow in such a stupid way that it was embarrassing to watch: a beech stick was flying in her hands like a whip, as though she were nearly thwacking someone; from under her colorful skirt an undershirt with a torn hem peeked out; a greasy waistcoat covered the wide shoulder straps of her shirt, and on her uncombed head a triangular gauze headscarf was thrown that was an indistinct color—but closer to what once had been white.

Iryna screamed so that you would think a column of evacuation carts was going along the street: her words got stuck in her mouth as though they had stumbled on stones. And if anyone didn't know, they would say that from her manner of speaking Iryna was Tsvychkov's sister.

As a matter of fact, before the conversation, or rather, the three-sided argument between Ivan, Iryna, and her nearby neighbors even started, a rather important detail (especially for the young women) was cataloged in the heads of the people: *Ivan Tsvychok was sleeping in a separate bed from sweet Darusya.*

Disillusioned, Varvara yawned, Yilena was relieved, and Maria was sympathetic.

While the matter of who was sleeping with whom and where was becoming clearer for the women, Ivan returned to the shed, got dressed, combed the hay out of his hair, and stood before Iryna with his pitchforks. His tongue also began to poke around between his teeth.

"Why have you, *gazda*, from early morning drawn a veil over your head? Have you thought about giving yourself to marriage again in your old age? Why are you screaming—has your tongue gotten tangled? Look, no one will take you because you're all wrinkled."

And he burst into laughter that could be heard all around the livestock pen. Iryna began to choke from such unexpected effrontery:

"You awful abomination, you stupid moocher,[19] you infertile seed, you, worst of fools, who came to live with a girl just as stupid as he is, you Galician bandit, you wretched wretch... I'll find justice for you, because such a person hasn't been born that I haven't found justice for... you'll be sitting in jail for your villainy—your bones will rot in jail...."

Only a man made of wood would have been able to listen further to the very colorful monologue of the brigade leader's wife. And Tsvychok was an animated man, so he boldly started at Iryna with his pitchforks, as if he were going to stick her onto the prongs right away and toss her to hell. But then and there right under her nose he changed tactics—he threw the pitchfork into the ground and grabbed the brigade leader's wife by the chest:

"What do you need from us, you snake?!"

"What do you mean what do I need?!" It nearly stuck in her throat. "What do you mean what do I need?! Give back the stolen headboard from my steel bed! You cajoled the child to steal half of my belongings from my house— and you dare ask what I need??!" Iryna sputtered and, it seemed, began to gasp from a lack of air.

Oh, no. A while back, as old folks tell the story, in the first war an entire army of cavalry rode through this village, and at the front of it Chapaev[20] or Brusilov[21] himself was riding on a white horse;

19   Literally a "priimak" is someone, who is "accepted" into his wife's family's house to live there.

20   Vasily Chapaev (1887-1919), a well-known Red Army commander and Soviet cultural hero, whose exploits were described in Dmitry Furmanov's novel *Chapaev* (1923), which was later released as a popular film under the same name in 1934.

21   Russian General Aleksei Brusilov (1853-1926) whose army operated in Galicia and in the Carpathian Mountains.

between the two wars Romanian troops trotted through with gifts, horse hooves churning up the dust of two neighboring villages and half a village from the other Polish side;

the Hungarians with rooster feathers sticking out of their hats and torn footcloths and bast shoes pranced into the second war on horses—

but this was the kind of flint sparking between stones on the road and horse hooves, as now were between Iryna's tongue and her teeth—there had been nothing like it before.

Iryna made one—strategic!—mistake, by calling Tsvychok a thief.

As you already know, he was called all kinds of things in the villages of Bukovyna and Halychyna, but not even a drunk would be bold enough to call him a thief. So that linguistic temerity now cost the brigade leader's wife the gauze headscarf torn from her head by Varvara and trampled underfoot as well as Maria's two fists, not so much into her waistcoat as much as into her shoulders.

Tsvychok in the meantime stood in front of Iryna, holding her arms to her sides, and asked forcefully:

"Just tell the truth, snake, because if you lie—you'll die here on the spot! Where was your steel headboard?"

"What do you mean where was it?! Behind the stable, on the bank where our part of the village dumps trash! But that steel headboard is ours, we were going to fence off the chicken coop with it!"

"Go home, you old slut, cook your husband some corn meal and keep your trap shut! Otherwise!" Ivan pulled out his pitchfork from the ground and shook it in front of the brigade leader's wife's eyes, after which she moved from the yard with her head uncovered, leaving the scythe at someone's feet.

In this way, the show in Darusya's yard ended without any bloodletting or any serious blows.

While the neighbors energetically discussed the morning row, Ivan quietly went into the house, walked up to Darusya, still half-stuck through the window, who was looking at the peoples' heads, pressed her to his chest in front of them, and tenderly stroked her head.

He whispered something into her ear, and even when universal silence reigned in the world, no one would have made out the words that Ivan Tsvychok said to sweet Darusya. Right after that she crawled back from the window, closed the shutters and began to build the fire in the stove.

...But the adventures with the steel didn't end in Cheremoshne this time.

Sometime around midday, the office door of the director of the eight-grade school opened up with a racket and rattling—and Dmytro Odainy tumbled and rolled across the threshold. He was the collective farm's warehouse keeper, whom in the village they called Member Roly-Poly[22] for his squat and round figure, as well as for his excessive use of the word "member."

"Mr. Director!" Without greeting him, Odainy thundered in a basso profundo. "Either manage your pupils, or the Party's District Committee will be managing you. You know that I'm a member of the District Committee and won't tolerate a member of the District Committee's

---

22   Kolobok is the name of a large round-headed nursery rhyme personage who also became popular in Russian cartoons.

office propagating such a mess in this school. That's the way it is!" And he slammed his fist on the director's desk.

The director—a tall young man in sunglasses—continued sitting at the desk, flipping the pages of a class attendance book.

"What's the hoo-ha with you, Mr. Member of the District Committee?" He raised his eyes over the rim of his glasses.

"With me?" Odainy was surprised. "This is your hoo-ha, because yesterday your pupils, instead of looking for scrap metal in the village and turning it in, robbed my own yard and carried off tons of metal to the yard of those two dumbos—Tsvychok and sweet Darusya. And you ask me what's the hoo-ha with me, may lightning strike you for that kind of upbringing!"

It makes no sense to relate the further conversation of Member Roly-Poly with the school director, because shortly after that, the door of the director's office opened up again and, escorted in by the village district policeman Stepan, who held a revolver in his right hand, Ivan Tsvychok crossed the threshold and took off his hat before those present:

"Good health to you, Mr.-Comrade Director!" He snapped abruptly.

The director looked at the district policeman, who hypnotized Tsvychok with his gaze, and Odainy shifted his eyes like a rat among all of them. The director started to laugh:

"Stepan, have you brought Ivan in to school to finish the eighth grade?"

"I've brought in a thief!" The policeman proudly fired off.

"What do you think I have here—a school or the district police department?" The director was surprised.

"But it was Ivan yesterday who urged your pupils to gather up the scrap metal into the yard of that stupid woman. She's not responsible; he's the one who's responsible. For the stealing of state treasure and for robbery in broad daylight inside the village. For violation of the passport code. This citizen is living here without a passport. He's a beggar; he disturbs the peace. He cohabitates with a female outside of the court's authority. He should be sent to jail. "

Tsvychok crumpled the hat in his hands and smiled in a really stupid way: the nonsense Stepan was talking would make a dead man laugh, not to mention Ivan.

"Wait!" The director interrupted nearly in a shout. "Ivan, explain what they want from you."

"They want a knot on their head, and a Romanian beech switch on their ass. That's what they want."

"But still…."

"I wish these ruffians would do some good deed instead of startling kids with their screaming."

"What deed, Ivan?"

"The thing is, Mr. Director, that there isn't a good man in charge in our village. Iron is lying all over in trenches, on the riverbanks and all the way to the club. Somebody's work is lost for nothing, and," he directed his eyes at the policeman, "this one with the gun doesn't see it. But Ivan Tsvychok must see this. And must see that in our so noble village and with such noble men there's no one to put a fence around the grave and cut the grass in the cemetery. So Ivan asked the schoolchildren to each make a sweep of the village and gather up steel pipes and a few rusted springs from old beds to put a fence around ill-fated Darusya's father's little house. That is all that Ivan did. Ivan will clean the pipes, polish them, weld the fence together at the blacksmith's—it will be nice to come to the cemetery. And it will be tidier in the village.

And these stallions have the nerve to attack a poor girl! Even though she's mute, she's ten times smarter than these smarty-pants. Now you can take me to the police office, then I'll tell them how much this member steals in the collective farm and where he hides it. Let him try to call Darusya foolish one more time!

And you, Mr. Director, when you stick up for an innocent soul, you'll be commemorated; you're a Christian, and not an atheist." And he slammed the door.

It was obvious from all this that Tsvychok had his full say in the director's office for three years in advance.

"Odainy!" The director said after a bit. "Where were those iron sideboards?"

"Where...," it wasn't clear whether Mr. Roly Poly was repeating the question or affirming it. "Behind the woodshed. I needed to throw them away on the riverbank because they were really rusty."

"So why are you steamed up about thievery?"

"Have you heard whose grave he's planning to fence off?! If it were for some *gazda*, but for... for shame."

"Odainy, fortunately even we'll end up where the guy is lying for whom your bed has become a gate... How awful and difficult people have now become!"

Tsvychok again opened the door at that moment and stuck his head through it. He, apparently, was standing in the corridor and listening the entire time.

"It's not that they've become that way, Mr. Director," Ivan said. "The people always were and will remain bad until they become quite miserable. As long as things are good—the people are bad. That's why they attack the weak. And I won't let them!" Tsvychok chopped at the air with his hand and stepped out of the office. And after a while, having discarded the waste, and after having cleaned and sorted the iron, Tsvychok took it in several wheelbarrows to the village blacksmith Petro and said straight away:

"Petro, I'm going to help you, and you're going to build a fence for Dovbush!"

"How?" The blacksmith threw his black hands into the air. "From this scrap metal?! Better not to have any than old and different kinds of it!"

"You're being really smart-alecky now, Petro!" He scolded the blacksmith. "And why haven't you helped a poor invalid earlier with something new and good? Have you been waiting for Ivan Tsvychok? I know my way around old metal, but I can't make it look good, not from different pieces. That's why I came to you! So, you figure out how to do it!"

When the fence for Darusya's father's grave was ready, the school director released five boys from class and sent them to help Tsvychok.

And on that day after Tsvychok managed to put a latch on the fence, Darusya spent the night at her father's grave. Her dogs waited at the gate—but not long enough, then trudged along the yards and backstreets. But Ivan sat there by the gate, wrapped up in the blanket that Darusya had left.

...Then one day Maria wiggled her finger to call over Tsvychok across the picket fence to her livestock pen. She took him behind the stable, looked around a few times to check whether anyone was eavesdropping. And then she whispered right into his ear:

"Ivan, I really beg you: don't ever bring Darusya any candies. Ever! And don't even ever show them to her."

Ivan looked strangely at Maria, fixed her scarf, and answered loudly:

"*I'm not stupid, I know... There are good people here— they've told me...,*" and he returned to his place.

*

Few people, maybe even no one in the wide world knew that Ivan's mouth would never keep shut around Darusya. Ivan putters around close to the house—and talks endlessly. What he sees, he talks about—he conducts a tour for Darusya. Even if she had been blind, he so clearly narrated that she could imagine everything happening around her. Ivan keeps narrating in a quiet voice, as though he's stroking Darusya on her head, and also points with his hand.

And it's as if she comes alive to his voice: and walks in a straighter line, and in the tiny corner of her lips a wrinkle appears, as though from a hidden smile, and the main thing is—her head stops aching.

But Tsvychok is Tsvychok: he was born for the *drymba* and rambling. He isn't able to sit in one spot. Then Ivan carries firewood to the house piled nearly all the way up to the ceiling, fills all the buckets, cans, and tubs with water, tells Darusya not to do anything too hard, and not to listen to anyone stupid, but just to Maria, and roams off with his *drymbas*, changes buses and hits different roads. The only way to find out where Ivan was just was from people who said they saw him either in Yaremche, or Bahno, or near Vashkivtsi, or next to Snyatyn.

In a week he rides the length and breadth of half the world—and brings home a bag of iron and presents for Darusya.

"Maria, would you be able to ride like Tsvychok where the bus rides or the railway goes? He once says he was ridin' to Vyzhnytsya, but somethin' happened that he ended up in Chornovets."

"I can't, but I'd want to, my silver Varvarka. Many a man would want to ride alone... Ivan is a free man. He does what his conscience lets him and his soul desires. We only do what we have to do."

...While Ivan is away, Darusya gets weak, like the dried out pear tree in her garden. She lies in the house with her head wrapped more and more often now, and she doesn't kindle a fire in the stove, she just laps up old, cold borsht, and nibbles stale bread. And when her head lets go of her—she stands by the gate and looks along the street the entire day.

She waits.

Either with her bare heels she senses when he's about to approach, or something else tells her that Ivan is already nearby, but Darusya almost always precisely right before his arrival ties up a little, white kerchief on her head and opens the wicket gate wide open, which for such an occasion is decorated with white flowers made of paper, in the way that gates are decorated for a wedding.

And a miracle happens: Ivan pops out from behind the corner, like a May mushroom—a spongy morel—after a rain: so unexpectedly, suddenly, that you aren't able to see when it happens.

Once Ivan was walking from the bus along with Mykola Hryhorkiv, who, like a woman, loved to judge everyone and give advice. Then Mykola got worked up:

"Ivan, tell me somethin'. In the village they say a he-fool is sleeping with a she-fool...."

"You, Mykola, are a fool yourself," Tsvychok snapped back, not thinking long and not waiting for the conversation to continue.

"No, you first hear me out ... Though you're stupid, sorry for using the word, but you are smart sometimes. See, you make the *drymbas*, sell them. You're a bit of a *gazda*. It means you're not completely stupid. You'd be better off moving in with some smarter young woman, one who'd start talking kindly to you, who'd warm you, and here you sleep in the shed like a homeless dog, and even cook for yourself. Why'd you need that Darusya? She's no use to a man. If she'd die on you, you'd have to look for a veil, cause you'd have to bury her like a virgin. But who's going to check after she dies if she's a virgin or not... Eh-h-h... what can you say—if she's weak in the head—what can you expect from her?"

"You should be ashamed to talk this way about an orphan, *gazda*!" Tsvychok shook his head. "You have your own three maidens in your house, it's better for you to keep your eyes on them, and don't tend to someone else... And who's told you, Nykolai, that Darusya's weak in the head? If her head aches—that doesn't mean she doesn't have lots of smarts. Well, take a look, some young women in the village do things from which you can see right away that they're weak in their head below the belt and in the head on their neck, and no one points a finger at them. And they're all in their right mind.

How can Darusya be stupid if she understands everything and does everything?! She washes my shirt! She cooks food. Yours feeds you the same buckwheat groats she feeds the dog, but Darusya adds mushrooms to her borsht for me. And adds honey to sour pickles. So how is she weak?! So she doesn't talk—because that's her fate. No one has ever outwitted his fate... Rather than say something stupid like these here people of ours, it's better for her to keep quiet. 'Cause there isn't anyone to talk to in this world, Nykolai....

And I want to tell you one last thing... There hasn't been a single woman who's been as good to me... not a one, and I've seen a bit of this life... and all of you say she's not smart."

*

...And once, having made a bag of *drymbas* and having sharpened some knives, Tsvychok said to Darusya:

"Let's get ready for the road. I'll show you the world. Let's see what do you have here?" And he began to go through her simple belongings, left still from her mother, and to her mother—from her grandmother. And so, Darusya's clothing is age-old. But Ivan shook off the dust, ironed the wrinkles with a wooden smoother, and began to get Darusya ready the way a father readies his daughter for a wedding.

For the road Ivan chose a plaid skirt with many pleats, a white, three-quarter-length-sleeved shirt with broad yellow-green patterns and light canvas shoes of undetermined age. He wrapped Darusya's head with two white kerchiefs himself, pushed a clove of garlic into her bosom and tied a red thread around her left arm (to ward off evil!)—then went with her arm-in-arm to the bus station.

Good Lord!

The village had seen everything. Young women crazed with love over someone else's husband came to blows and uttered vile insults; honorable maidens of *gazdas* without a marriage wreath carried children born of lechery under their hems; out of jealousy the richest *gazda* in the village set fire to his own house, setting his wife's clothing on fire on the floor in the middle of the bedroom; a bride-to-be ran away right before registering her wedding on her wedding day; fathers had to rear someone else's children like their own; but there hadn't been a similar response in Cheremoshne as on that day when Tsvychok accompanied sweet Darusya on his arm to the bus station!

The women left their rising dough to run out through their kneading troughs, the men tossed down their axes and pitchforks, children ran out from their classes, when Ivan in a narrow summer hat with a chicken feather and a tiny round mirror stuck behind the brim, in his only white shirt, in his flared pants fashionable about ten years ago, and in a long waistcoat, like an opera conductor's, and a plaid kerchief around his neck, walked with Darusya on his arm along the village street, whistling either "The Hutsul Girl"[23] or a waltz. And Darusya was somehow bashfully looking at her feet—as if she were floating next to Ivan, like a princess, from time to time fixing the hair beneath her kerchiefs.

...Till today the world for Darusya ended beyond the village mill that stood on the very edge of Cheremoshne.

She remembers a long time ago when every day with her mother she used to walk along the riverbank, morning and evening, in the hope of getting rid of the stifling cough, from which she suffered so much. The neighbors said to cure whooping cough with air from the river and coltsfoot tea mixed with dried corn silk. Darusya couldn't drink the bitter infusions—in the wee hours of the morning she dragged her mother to the river—and they ever so quietly minced along the riverbank all the way to this now old mill, and then came back.

Dampness wafted from the river and the fog spread. Somewhere sheep were bleating and dogs yelping, but Darusya kept holding her mother's hand—and the cough let go of her little throat, and she breathed in the sharp air—it even took her breath away. And it was easier for her, and good, because father was waiting for her at home; he lifted Darusya up into his arms, tossed her above his head and she screamed—to the point that Maria wagged her head from behind the wicket fence:

"Shame on you, man, do you want to terrify the child?!"

In her life Darusya never walked further than the mill. Maybe once long ago with Maria one time she went to the neighboring village to the cemetery. She never wanted to

23   For a demonstration of "The Hutsul Girl" dance, see: http://www.youtube.com/watch?v=KR0iiXoymRU.

anymore. People got drunk at the graves; they growled, and Darusya's head also aches from the growling.

…People think Ivan's a fool, but he did it his own way: he's brought Darusya by cart from Cheremoshne to Kuty. How he made arrangements in every village always with a different driver—God only knows. Either he passed out new horseshoes to the drivers for free, or his unabating *drymba* did its work, but Tsvychok sat Darusya down next to himself, put into her hands an open parasol, in truth, it was filled with holes, to shade her from the sun—and the horses took them into the world, which from birth Darusya had never seen. They reached Kosiv by bus around lunchtime.

And Tsvychok, quickening his pace, took Darusya straight to the district clinic. It was evident they also knew Ivan here: the nurses teased him with a gentle "Where's your *drymba*, Ivan?" or "Is this your wife, Ivan?" And they whispered further among themselves in the corridors, without particularly inquiring into what he strove to say in answer.

Ivan had enough of this kind of business, and not letting go of Darusya's hand, he opened the door to one of the offices straight away. A young doctor in a white coat, smiling into his slight whiskers, looked for a long time at the strange pair, and then said:

"How can I help you, sir."

"She's not mute," Ivan turned to Darusya and nearly forcibly sat her onto a chair opposite the doctor. "But she doesn't talk. I want you to make it so she speaks. Because her head hurts from that." And he placed two *drymbas* on the doctor's desk and a new hexagonal file.

"Well, well...," the doctor stood up from behind the desk and sat down—knee to knee—right in front of Darusya. "And who are you?" he asked Ivan.

"What do you mean who? A person! Ivan!" Tsvychok was surprised. "You look at her, and not at me. I speak badly because I'm tongue-tied, but I talk anyway, and she understands everything, and hears, but stays silent. And people have said to me, you have some kind of hypnosis... or you can just cut something out, because I might pass away, and who will help her then?.."

You don't even have to say more, because the young doctor was the district infectious disease specialist and dietician in one person. He didn't even think of getting involved in Darusya's case, especially, when in answer to his question, whether they had been in a psychiatric hospital, Tsvychok spat at the doctor's feet "You need to go to a psychiatric hospital." They both were from a different district and even from a different oblast. To add to that, they didn't have any documents on them. Darusya looked at the doctor with her big, intelligent eyes—and it seemed to him that she was hypnotizing him. But now throughout the villages there are so many gypsies and all kinds of charlatans who hoodwink people when they can, and the doctor's entire monthly pay was in his pocket. The neurologist that day had a day off. The otolaryngologist was on vacation. So the doctor took one of Ivan's *drymbas* because he knew how to play it, took another one at the same time with a file and put it in the pocket of Ivan's dress coat, started to laugh, and said:

"Ivan, it's better for you to sell *drymbas*... It's more useful for you. And this one," he pointed his finger at Darusya, "is mute. Don't mess with her head." And the doctor made the crazy sign with his finger by his head: "She's weak in the head just like you, my man. And no one can help her here. Or anywhere."

"Your mother was a whore!" Tsvychok screamed in the doctor's face. "If you don't want to treat her, then I'm going to treat her myself, and may you be tormented by your conscience, like the worst wretch... It's not for nothing people say bad things about you. Sometimes people say the truth about people like you... Be well, but remember that you have children and grandchildren. And there's no guarantee the same thing won't happen to them." And he slammed the door so hard that it popped open again.

...And after the Feast of Peter and Paul,[24] the village was turned upside down over Ivan and Darusya: Varvara, who had the nickname *Zlodiyka*—the She-Thief—attached to her, passed along the news almost from house to house—she was almost choking from impatience.

"*Holy-holy-holy...*[25] *My good golden friend,*[26] *they bathe naked as jaybirds in the greenhouse in the middle of the night facing the moon, and aren't ashamed that the village is asleep... but they defile the village... and huddle together, for sure, in the water... the house isn't enough for them... the police should deal with them... good people, who has seen such a thing in our time?!*"

---

24   On July 12.

25   The three beginning words of the people's response in part of the Holy Anaphora of the Liturgy of John Chrysostom: "*Holy, holy, holy, Lord Sabaoth, heaven and earth are filled with Your glory. Hosanna in the highest. Blessed is He who comes in the name of the Lord. Hosanna to God in the highest.*" Varvara seems to be warding off evil by repeating the words from the liturgy.

26   *Kumka* in the original. It is the diminutive form for the word *kuma*,

"And you, Varvara, aren't you ashamed to go to your Petro at night when your husband is right nearby? If you didn't hang around where you don't need to, and stayed around the house, then you might not see what, maybe, never happened...."

*

It was like this. Ivan noticed that the water would save Darusya from weakness, that often times she would get her legs wet up to her knees in the river—to the point that the skin on her legs would wrinkle like dried fruit after it's smoked in a wooden cooker—and got lost in thought. He kept on thinking and thinking—and made up his mind.

He perfected the process, the smarty-pants of today would say.

One night when the entire village was snoring at the top of its lungs, and even the dogs were dozing in their doghouses, Ivan took Darusya by the hand and went with her to the greenhouse.

A round moon hung above the water and reflected in the thick willow branches; grasshoppers sang excitedly; blue and green frogs croaked and blinked their eyes—and Tsvychok, undressing completely, but covering his shame with the palm of his hand, plopped into the water that was as warm as the milk squeezed from a cow. He swam not particularly deftly, but he swam. Then, standing up to his navel in the water, he quietly called out to Darusya: "Come here and don't be afraid. Get un-

---

which has multiple meanings in Ukrainian from godmother of someone or someone's child to a close, intimate friend or crony.

dressed—and go completely into the water up to your head. You'll see—this will help you—and he turned his back to the shore so as not to embarrass poor Darusya, who was already holding her skirt in her hands.

Darusya went into the water in her undershirt with wide breech bands. When the water reached her knees, she stopped.

Ivan looked at her and remained silent.

After standing there a bit, Darusya went further.

Ivan moved toward her, until the water reached his chest. They stood like that—both up to their chest in the water, facing each other, with arms stretched forward, as though they had the intention to throw themselves at each other in an embrace.

The moon quivered on the silver watery path between them, the wind quietly played in the grass—and Ivan led Darusya by the hand until the water reached their chins.

"See how good it is? Splash around a little just like me, this way, that way... And don't be afraid—I'm holding you. Feel that, how easy it is? And now dive with your head... like this—oh-h-h...," he snorted, spitting out water through his nose and mouth. "Wet your head... like this... all of it... wet it again... Lord, how smart you are, Darusya...."

And on the shore Ivan wrapped her legs and shoulders, combed her hair with his fingers, rubbed her hands, thought something, and in wide steps nearly ran to a hollowed out log trough filled with drinking water.

Good people... How good it is that sometimes in life moments happen, that not a single soul knows about, other than the person, who with his own hands, creates that moment!...

Ivan scooped out of the hollowed out log trough handfuls of healthy, cold water and gave Darusya a drink like a little child, not spilling a single drop so it wouldn't chill her breasts.

...And at home what was supposed to happen in such a situation between a healthy man and a healthy woman happened.

However, Ivan knew: Darusya is smart, but not completely healthy.

And he did what in his opinion wouldn't cause her harm.

Almost to dawn (how long can the night until Petrivka[27] be) the naked Darusya lay on top of a warm shawl, spread out on the bedcover by Ivan, and he looked at her—and nearly cried, whispering into her ear some kind of wondrous vinaigrette of words, sobs, sighs and wails, that whoever did not learn to understand the rattling of Tsvychok's tongue between his gum and palate, would think that he was singing through the gnashing of teeth.

"Are you a virgin, Darusya?" He asked her to her face, and then, lowering his gaze, answered the question himself. "A virgin, just look, whose desires have beaded up on your brow. But you can't make love with a man. Do you hear me? You can't. You need to, but can't. Be careful not to fall for men. They're such bastards—they'll molest...," he wanted to say 'a cripple,' but he bit his tongue, "a chaste maiden, and the fact that she's a poor orphan won't stop them. And they'll knock you up.

I'd get you pregnant myself. Want me to? Look what a tight belly you have." He outlined her stomach with his

27 Petrivka, as it's called in the Ukrainian folk tradition, comprises the

palm. "You'd carry a baby well, and in your old age you'd have someone to care for you... But no, I'm not going to get you pregnant. How will you teach it to speak? I'll kick the bucket, and they'll take away the child to a boarding school. It'll be an orphan. You shouldn't. I'll get someone else pregnant... Somebody stupid. But not you... Listen to me carefully, Darusya. You understand everything, then listen: avoid men.

Lordy-Lordy... And what if desire comes to you? And if I'm no longer in your life? I can't live forever, I could die tomorrow, what would you do? No, stay a virgin till your death... it's not shameful.

...And you are healthy. Don't listen to anyone. You're healthier than this entire stupid village. But I don't want to have it on my conscience, because you're a total orphan and your fate is unhappy. You're punished by fate... And if desire for you comes from a man, they'll pass you from one man to another... no, it's better for you not to know a man....

You see, I don't really often need a woman. And you would need a man to keep from getting sick.[28] And I don't want you to wail like a wounded she-wolf without me. But someone else will wrong you... wrong you for sure...."

...Who knows... maybe in such a way people chosen by nature or God become psychotherapists, seers, prophets, priests, blessèd, icon painters. Right at such moments when we sincerely wish a person good and aid, do we believe in them ourselves and thus heal them?!

1-5 weeks of time of fasting following Easter and before the church holiday of Sts. Peter and Paul. The time is associated with ancient fertility rights. For more information on it see: http://www.ukrlit.vn.ua/habits/n50lz.html.

28   The author has explained this to me as the folk belief that a woman receives positive energy from her husband by his presence next to her that wards off illness.

...Darusya lay there with her eyes shut listening to Ivan—and suddenly she got goose bumps all over her body. Fine ones, like bubbles on the smooth surface of a summertime river, when the rain suddenly begins—a flash rain. Her every vein and particle of blood quivered—and then Darusya suddenly understood for herself that she's not stupid—but as sweet, as that sweet trembling-fever that she never had known. Ivan's rumbling whispering burst through the constant fog in her head, it made its way somewhere so deep and far that Darusya didn't suspect that there were such places inside her. At that moment she didn't have any shame or fear—just a super thin thread, like the moon's path on the water of the greenhouse, quivered between her and Ivan, and called her pained soul to go fearlessly to that call... And when Ivan's calloused hands pressed the soft flat surface of Darusya's womb grown numb—a moan or a howling escaped from her, or a celebration of joy—such a thing that could swallow half a world beneath her ... Lordy-Lordy... she had been mute for a quarter century until she felt in herself the embryos of a living, forgotten language near her father in the cemetery... but now, under Ivan's hands she did begin to speak. In a coarse, inhuman voice, similar to the roar of a wounded beast or the efforts of a simultaneously mute, deaf and sightless person, but she began to speak in words, in words long ago denied by her tongue and throat. This was some kind of wild guttural impasse and hope at the same time, gratitude and an appeal, damnation and laughter...

Then Ivan began to cry. Shameful male tears rolled along Tsvychok's unshaven face and dripped on Darusya's burning hot breasts—and she, gathering all her strength, will and anger, answered him: "I-van…."

For the sake of this nocturnal moaning he would have crawled from the edge of the world to Darusya's—and now his—house.

But after that night he knew the main thing: Darusya could be cured. How—Ivan didn't know, but he knew precisely that she could.

The attacks of pain tormented her less and less.

Sometimes—though it was rare—she could even smile.

And once Ivan even thought he could marry Darusya.

He took the *drymba* to his lips, sat on the threshold of the porch, played for a long time, looked at Darusya with her arms crossed under her breasts, and kept thinking … and thinking… What torments you need to endure to live this life… not to know a man, not even to have periods, to hear only evil things from people and not to have affection from anyone, besides maybe Maria?! Not to be able to cry, to sob, to scream yourself blue, to laugh, but to be a living mummy and to have in your head a large wound, as though caused by a bullet, and not to be able to talk about it, but just to think and keep thinking. Someone else would have long ago forgotten, but she, poor girl, punishes herself like that great martyr Kateryna[29]….

And then lo and behold: Tsvychok refused to go on his usual trips. He made his *drymbas* and passed them along through someone to the bazaar at Kosiv or Kuty, but he now rarely left Darusya alone. Now he was afraid that these spiteful and wicked people, who were more

---

29   The 4th century St. Catherine of Alexandria, who converted to Christianity and served to convert many others. She remained a virgin and was known for her great intellect and beauty. She was condemned to death and beheaded by Roman Emperor Maxentius.

concerned with the lives of others than with their own, would distress her.

When Ivan went to someone's place for a day of paid labor he would take Darusya with him, sit her down in the shade, give her beans or corn to shuck, and he would either chop wood or mow, or put together pole fences, and his hands would sing without music.

...But it's true that it's not as bad for anyone as for our enemies when things are going well for us.

Then you don't need either the evil eye or sorcery. Just a single tongue that knows how to turn in the mouth would do, and people would add the rest....

"Did you hear, Maria... Either those dogs, the ones that walk behind Darusya to the cemetery, or wolves are howling at night from their house. These two fools have dinner at the table together with the dogs. Your hair stands on end.

"And you, golden Varvarka, don't walk near someone else's walls and you won't seem to hear the wolves. Keep to your own household. There's something no less interesting to hear there. And don't talks down to the crippled. Even if they're having supper with dogs, so what of it? They're not taking any food from your plate."

"You never see light there! And they sleep with the dogs in one bed, the two fools. Oy, dear friend, I'll call the police."

"But the dogs don't come to your place, why do you need the police?"

"For the sake of justice."

"Have you heard, my dear friend, an evil spirit has appeared in the village. At the cemetery and at Darusya's house. From the time Ivan Tsvychok started to live with her, that's when the evil spirit settled among the people...."

"And what does that evil spirit do, Vasylynka, that it gives you no peace?"

"What does it do… It's affected sweet Darusya. And what if it affects the entire village?!"

"Oy, my dear friend, it ain't likely there's a spirit on earth that could change you…."

"Sins… the reason for everything is sins, my dear friend… unrepented sins and the tears of the dead… But why should the sins of others befall us?"

"Nothing bad has befallen you, dear friend, so why are you getting so worked up?!"

"Because I don't know what's happening in that damn house, and I live nearby. So I get worked up for the sake of my peace of mind and justice."

*

O-O-O… Not just people, but Satan too gets on edge when things go better for someone a little longer than he intends.

Even simple people, who believe in God, who prepare for communion and keep the fast, who teach their children to obey and to say the 'Our Father,' who remember the dead and care for the future of their children, introduce a correction to Satan's plans."

No-no, no Satan has the kind of power that simple people have in a time of envy, hate, and revenge….

…And one day Ivan Tsvychok was called into the village council.

The puffed up head of the council sprawled out from behind the desk like an overgrown cornmeal kasha oozing out of a short cast iron pot.

The district policeman Stepan from time to time slapped his holster on his pants, as if each time he were checking that his weapon were in place.

And near the wall, leaning her head low over papers, sat the secretary of the village council Dusya, constantly blowing her nose from a midsummer head cold.

The head of the council tapped his fingers on the desk, twisted his moustache as if he wanted to make a cigarette from it, and looking past Tsvychok, asked:

"What's going on at night there at your place, Ivan?"

Ivan stood by the door and crumpled his hat. You wouldn't say he was frightened. But he didn't seem calm in the least. Obviously, he was thinking, but he was thinking slowly.

Ivan's manner of thinking long didn't seem strange to those who were planning to write a report right then: among the village council Tsvychok was considered one of the dim ones, because besides the fact that he had moved in with dim Darusya, he also made *drymbas* with such intensity, the way normal people in the summer make hay or, in the winter, children; he always speaks loudly—you hear him at the other end of the village, and once he says something—it would be easier to endure someone spitting in your eye than listen to that... And my Lord! He had so many signs of a half-wit that you didn't have to beat around the bush with him. But the Soviet government is just: for it everyone is equal. And everyone is equal before the law. The people think Tsvychok is dim, but he doesn't have a certificate from the psych ward. So the law applies to him as it does to anyone else. Just so!

…Ivan didn't know the Stanislavsky method, but he remained silent for a long time. Longer than the silence in the last scene of Gogol's *The Inspector General*. Then he sat across from the head of the council, leaned over the desk—and quietly, unlike himself, very quietly, started to jabber with his tied tongue:

"Tell me, Mr. Head, why would you care about me here in your village council? You think I'm not brimming with smarts, but I'm just not brimming with happiness. But I don't sponge off anyone… I've never robbed anyone, haven't broken any windows, kicked up a row in the village, or disgraced a single girl. I'm soon gonna be fifty. They won't take me into the army… so there wasn't a reason to call me into the village council. So what if I don't have my own house, then why'd you so intelligent people and your so intelligent government take away my mother's house after she died from beatings at the Ministry of State Security, and then cut me loose to live by begging?"

"That's not the point, Ivan!" Stepan interrupted him. "And we didn't beat your mother, or take her house."

"People like you took it… And you can beat a person with something other than beech switches! And all this is to the point. Why have you summoned me here?! Obviously, you don't have more important work in the village than to pick on a cripple. So tell me fast what you want from me, 'cause my farmstead is there without its working hands right now. They bring everything to your house in carts and wagons, but I have to make it with my calluses, to feed myself and the orphan Darusya."

A beet cooked for borsht has less of a crimson color than the face of the head of the village council had at that instant:

"What are you, fool, wagging your tongue here? We'll take you to the police station right now for fifteen days—you'll start talking there...."

"I'll tell a lot here, for sure... About you. Shtefan, I'll tell about how when you're drunk you chase after other men's young women with a gun... and how your wife makes home brew from the collective farm's sugar... you can have no doubt about that... Ivan will tell everything...." Ivan jumped up from the chair, sharply pushed it right to the door. "What do you, bulls, need from the two of us? Tell me, because I'm dim—I can toss this chair into your head!"

The head of the council along with the district police officer scratched the back of their heads, led out the secretary, and stood before Ivan as though on the final line before an assault. They talked in turn, counting, evidently, on the effectiveness of the psychological attack:

"We ask you one more time: what happens at your house at night that makes people complain and demand that we examine your conduct at a session of the village council?"

"The house is by the road—people aren't deaf."

"Everything bad that's happened in the village is tied to you, Ivan."

"Before you appeared here—Darusya was normal. She'd dig herself into the earth...."

"Tied up pear trees...."

"Walked through the village with dogs...."

"And now she's stopped going to the cemetery... Doesn't go to see her father."

"She listens to your *drymba* and brings the dogs together in the house at night."

"…You should leave our village, Ivan."

Then Ivan spattered both of them in the face with his saliva from standing too close, but, for some reason, they didn't wipe it off:

"Do you know what? If I feel like it, I'll die in your village, and you'll have to bury me here. And it's none of your damn business what happens in someone else's house at night. What needs to is happening. Let a person live peacefully at least in their own four walls!"

"It'll be peaceful, Ivan, in the next world. But while we are the authority—we must know everything."

"I want to shit on this authority of yours that looks under peoples' covers! And if you bother Darusya with even a word—I'll cut off your heads like mangy curs, even if it means I'll rot in jail…."

*

… I would have been inexpressibly happy to end the story about sweet Darusya and Ivan Tsvychok on an optimistic note. Say, for example, that her protector finally appeared, who wouldn't allow anyone to raise a finger against the poor orphan; and that they began to live in peace and quiet; and the pain disappeared for Darusya; only her voice didn't return; but that didn't prevent them from amusing each other at least with trivial little things, to which a person in his everyday life would never pay attention, the way that a two-handed person never pays attention to his hands, and a two-legged person to his legs.

I'd be happy to… but well! Life, probably, like people, is vengeful over joy. And especially if the joy for two is great: the kind that it is for Ivan—Darusya's moaning beneath his hands, and for Darusya—Ivan's love and caring, which were taken away from her when cruel people gave her candy.

It's said: there never was such happiness, it's gone. And it's not needed.

Darusya's fate, perhaps, suddenly skipped away before Ivan... Perhaps it's jealous too?

...So they took away Tsvychok for fifteen days to the regional police center. First for resisting the authorities and their plenipotentiary representative during the conduct of their official duties, and second—for his attempt to take possession of a district police officer's weapon, and third—for profanity, and abasement of the honor and dignity of those present during a conflict on the premises of the village council. Date. Signatures. The end of the protocol.

Maybe that's what you get, Ivan, for being so wise around smart people!

Ivan was shaved bald as a billiard ball in the regional police center; instead of a *drymba*, they put an old broom into his hands—and Ivan went to sweep the streets of the regional center. It rained heavily—and washed away the dust, but Ivan, anyway, swept the broken road that had never been paved with asphalt. And in buses and cars people made the crazy sign near their heads and shrugged their shoulders, because it was the stupidest of stupidities especially here, in the mountains, to sweep the street.

And Ivan gave a report every day about what he did and counted the days till the end of his hellish torments.

Under the heavy rains his slim pants became torn and his really old shirt, probably Darusya's father's, that he had found in her shed, was covered in holes. And right before his return home, Tsvychok seriously became worried: in what will he show himself in front of Darusya?

But you come across good people everywhere. Even in the regional office of the police.

A sergeant, who for the entire fifteen days was the arrested man's supervisor, gave Ivan his nearly new army clothing: dark green slacks—riding breeches with ties around the ankles, a wide belt and a shirt, just as green and with shiny buttons. He was only missing boots and a cap. But Ivan was unspeakably happy for even such riches.

Thus, just as the door of the jail cell opened before him, hastily getting dressed and cleaning off his brown hat well along with his patched and repatched slippers, he got in the bus to Cheremoshne and for the first time in several days took the *drymba* to his mouth.

That's the way he walked from the bus station right to Darusya's house—playing the *drymba*.

...When poor Darusya caught sight of Ivan at the wicket gate, her eyes somehow strangely rolled—and she quietly slipped down to the ground, right into the dust.

While Ivan was pouring water on Darusya and carrying her into the house, Maria ran up. Sobbing, she wrung her hands, and then, repeating again and again, beat her head with her fists:

"Yoi! Ivan... Ivan... You should have never done it... yoi... I wish you hadn't."

Ivan, like a crazed man, shook Maria by the shoulders

in the yard and bellowed like a bull who was kept from going to his she-cow:

"What shouldn't I have done, Maria?! What? Tell me!"

Maria cried and shook her head, and then ran off to her house.

...Darusya's attack of headache pain lasted this time from the second Feast of the Blessed Virgin,[30] that's from the twenty-first of September, all the way until the Feast of the Protectress.[31] Over that time she grew thin and her complexion blackened, she became covered in some kind of tiny sores.

When she could sit down—she beat her head against the wall, so Ivan had to sit next to her constantly and hold her hands.

She didn't eat and just drank water with dry bread, and didn't look at Ivan a single time, and only let Maria wrap her head. She lay turned away to the wall, with her eyes covered with scarves, and would just ceaselessly crumple the corner of the bed cover.

Ivan carried Darusya in his arms like a child to the greenhouse. He held her beneath her underarms in the water—but it didn't give her any relief.

He tried to heal her with smoke and then gave her water to put out the fire.[32]

He sprinkled her bed with holy water.

He brought in the priest and village nurse.

But Darusya just lay there, not reacting either to light or sound—she was just not dead.

---

30 The church Feast Day of the Nativity of the Virgin Mary on September 21 according to the Julian Calendar (September 8 by the Gregorian).

31 The Feast Day of the Protection (or Intercession) of the Virgin Mary is on October 14 (Julian Calendar) or on October 1 (Gregorian).

32 A folk ritual to cleanse someone of evil spirits causing their illness. Thanks to Olha Tytarenko for pointing this out.

"My heart feels you need to leave, Ivan…," Maria said to him sadly one day. "I'm sorry, it's not your fault…."

"I see that myself… But who's at fault, Maria?" Tsvychok cried without being embarrassed, and blew his nose with the edge of his old shirt, in which he had once split wood for Maria and in which he had come to Darusya.

"Fate, Ivan, and people. And no one else."

…Darusya got up on the second day after the Feast of the Protectress. She looked all around the house. She put Ivan's simple belongings in a bag. She wrapped up bread that Maria had brought in a white scarf, put the bread into Ivan's hands, and opened up the door to the porch in front of Ivan.

She strained for a long time, longer than a woman delivering her first child, but all the same she put the letters together in her throat, because barely audibly, so that only Tsvychok and not even Maria's cat next to Darusya's feet could hear, and said:

"…G-o-a-w-a-y I-v-a-n…."

She pointed her hand to the road and returned to the house.

Mykhailo's Miracle
The Main Drama

"**M**ykhailo sweetie, you should go have supper…." It's as though Matronka is asking, or perhaps requesting in a voice that resembles the rustling of a weasel in the hay; she stands on the porch in a white embroidered blouse with the sleeves rolled up to her elbow.

In the sunset September rays, her small head in a tightly plaited braid on her crown looked like a second sun rising among the fragrant pears, with which the entire porch was strewn all the way to the windowsill of the house. Matronka is laughing with just her roundish dimples, taking a bite of the honey pear, disturbing an entire swarm of wasps around her.

"Have you, my sweet darling, cooked something good today?" The man, in a Hutsul *keptar* sheepskin coat, its fur turned inside out, lifts his head from the chopping block without letting go of the ax in his hands.

The mountain of freshly split wood appears white and has the same clean scent as his wife's embroidered blouse in the setting sun.

For a moment both of them are silent, with their motionless eyes gazing at one another, as if they were to have a bite of each other just like that yellow, overripe pear that suddenly falls from his woman's hand and rolls its way to her man holding the ax. As though she's ashamed of some secret thought, the tiny woman shrivels, and then she places her hands on her hips:

"I've molded a fistful of cornmeal, one yellow like the sun, it laughs from its circle. May I be frozen on this spot till tomorrow if I'm tellin' a lie! If you don't believe me, go take a look yourself!" She answers cheerfully and disappears in the aperture of the door. And, lanky as a pole, Mykhailo, to whom you never have to say anything twice, carries the ax to the woodcutting area. He sweeps the path from the stable to the house with an old broom, brushes off his pants from the wood shavings and sawdust and goes to supper.

Matronka has already been waiting next to the wide wooden pail behind the stove with a pitcher of warm water and a towel tossed over her shoulder.

"Mykhailo sweetie, didn't I ask you not to split that wood late?" She reproaches him while helping him change his clothes.

Mykhailo takes off his *keptar* sheepskin coat and his shirt, and leans over the wooden pail with his half-naked body, placing his neck under the stream of water. Loudly snorting and laughing, he taps his wife's cheek with his wet hand:

"But why, can it cause harm?"

"But you, my silver sweetheart Mykhailo, were splitting the wood without your wide belt on, and the wind was strong, you might catch a cold in the small of your back. Who needs that?!"

Barely touching her husband's back with her hand, Matronka for some reason stops her trembling hand on a large birthmark under his right shoulder blade and circles around it with her forefinger. Next she quickly kisses him several times, and then wipes his shoulders with a handful of wet cotton and soap. After this Matronka starts to work on Mykhailo's chest, neck, and arms—and wipes them so diligently, as if her husband's body had not had water on it for years.

With eyes shut Mykhailo silently allows his wife's quick arms to turn him, dry him off, dress him in a clean shirt, and then, tousling Matronka's thick bangs, asks her in a feigned menacing tone:

"What did you say you cooked there, my sweet little *gazda*?"

"Just try it…," Matronka squinted slyly, while she was unwrapping a linen cloth from the cornmeal: yellow—like the sun—the polenta was steaming with white vapor.

There's nothing that Mykhailo loves more after a hard day's work than hot cornmeal with *brynza* sheep milk cheese. Matronka takes off the top with a wooden spoon, places the *brynza* cheese in the hollowed out part—it's almost the same yellow color as the corn meal—and then covers it again. She sits down across the table from her husband—and both of them wait until the oily cheese starts to melt in the butter and until it begins to flow through the yellow pores of the polenta.

Mykhailo and Matronka always have dinner the same way: sitting across from each other and leaning their foreheads against each other.

To onlookers it might seem that they don't want or aren't bold enough to look each other in the eye and, because of that, don't move their heads apart from each other over the course of dinner. On the other hand, to onlookers, it's quite evident that their hands somewhat shyly and hastily seek the opportunity to touch, but then just as hastily, as if they had been burnt or caught stealing, their hands separate quickly to their knees or along the tablecloth.

No one has ever seen Mykhailo and Matronka having dinner from outside since they tightly cover the windows and close the gate to the yard before dark, which no one in the village does. No one has ever seen this not because this young couple is stingy, unfriendly, or unwilling to have conversations with others. Other people for the time being simply weren't in a rush to visit them at their home: there had been no Baptism; they hadn't given birth to anyone; they hadn't paid respects to anyone at a funeral—no one in their two-person house had died; they didn't celebrate the church's patron saint's day just because they didn't do that. They lived like two porcini mushrooms in the forest under a beech tree, secretly, as though they were covered with moss and pine needles.

And besides that, as the village philosopher Tanasiy Maksymiuk said outside the church after their wedding ceremony: "Let these two make children now; after that they'll do work," then there was no way anyone would bother the young couple. There was also no need to ask for advice from such young people since they were the ones in need of advice. They didn't lend things to anyone because they have just gotten started in their household. And if they were somewhat bewildered in a world of their own after their wedding for a bit too long now, who doesn't that happen to? Especially when a lad takes an outsider, and not one of his own village girls, and examines her night and day from every side, like a *pysanka*,[33] decorated in a different village.

---

33 See footnote #4.

"B-a-n-g... Everything passes. And this shall pass," Tanasiy once blew into his pipe—and gave the final answer to the silent shrugs of the young women, who, with jealous looks, followed Mykhailo and Matronka when they would come to the Sunday service: she—with an invariably lowered head, as though from shame—quietly found a place on the women's side, and he—like a pole, stood out among the men. But their eyes all the same were tied as if with some kind of invisible string; and this so obviously struck others, that among the more experienced women, their nostrils flared from jealousy and unavoidable wonder like cows right before calving.

However the people's jealousy for these two bore no ill will.

For the time being....

*

...They call Matronka Mykhailo's wonder in the village. More precisely, Mykhailo gave her that nickname himself.

From early childhood Mykhailo Ilashchuk was a complete orphan. His father had been knocked over by a raft when the boy was twelve years old, and three years after that Mykhailo's mother went into the clay as the result of women's wagging tongues: the village women slandered her, saying that married *gazdas* were spending the night at the poor widow's. So two of the most jealous women of Cheremoshne quietly conspired. They took the woman to the forest since they knew no one would be looking for her, then tied her to a beech tree—and left her like that for the night to chill her desire. They found the widow the next day, chewed to the bone by wolves. No one was punished for it, because no one saw the abduction, but the entire village really knew the truth. But the village didn't testify, and there was no one to get to the truth, so the police closed the case. Thus the young Mykhailo hired himself out to other people, to eke out a living among the *gazdas*, learning various types of handyman work to make money. He led a bachelor's life for a long time until he managed to save up a bit of money for a small farmstead, for a teeny tiny of a complete orphan— just like himself—from another village and for their small wedding.

Maybe because he was an orphan, alone like a single finger, or maybe because the good Lord endowed him with this kind of nature, Mykhailo was a very polite and upright bachelor before he got married: he didn't seduce maidens; he didn't toss up young women's skirts; he didn't wallow in widows' feather beds. He was very capable of work and spoke very little. In public his tongue became untied just once—during "The Hutsul Girl" wedding dance, when his guests and those who came with the bride noisily filled the floor, and the music played so fast the fiddler's string broke.

Drunken from joy, Mykhailo with a slight movement placed onto his hand the petite bride—in height just about up to his bellybutton—Matronka, her name unusual for their village. He lifted her above his curly head, and turned her above him like a whirligig, to the point an older bridesmaid started to scream, having taken a fright, wringing her thin girlish hands.

"Guests! My dear guests enjoying yourselves, look at Mykhailo's wonder, admire Mykhailo's wonder, and long enjoy the company of Mykhailo's wonder! Gaze at Mykhailo's wonder!" With one hand he twirled her above the heads of the guests like a jubilant multi-colored flower.

The voice of the groom cracked, straining to interrupt the musicians, so it was not discernable whether he was really drunk, or just a little bit silly.

Because such a thing happened in this village when a groom lost his mind at his own wedding. Because of that old folks said: *the long abstinence of the flesh* is to blame for it, so to say, it wasn't necessary to wait for the wedding, but just go to a girl who asks for it and gives it herself, and an honest guy and his family wouldn't suffer grief to this day....

And Matronka, with her eyes shut either from fear or joy, clung to the neck of her young groom with both her thin arms, the way a child grabs her father, and in the frenzied tempo of "The Hutsul Girl," the colored ribbons in her hair wound around Mykhailo like a noose—it was terrifying she might strangle him.

Thus they danced that mad dance—just the two of them: the young groom, whose head nearly reached to the sky, and the young bride—her entire weightless tiny body grown into his supple male body, sturdy from constant work—wound her two arms around his neck and, barely conscious from not being used to it, from embarrassment of what was awaiting her beyond the gate of a new life in a different village, without her father and mother—just at the Lord's and her husband's bidding.

"I wish that it be all for the good, for the good ...," old women and young girls on benches next to the walls of the wedding house either judgmentally or sympathetically nodded their heads, as though they were looking into some book of fate, open just for them but invisible to everyone else. Or maybe they just extracted from the treasure chests of their own experience perfect knowledge about the future of the two newlyweds and people mute in their happiness, who slowly came to their senses after "The Hutsul Girl."

"For the good! For the good!" Mykhailo immediately answered all the female *gazdas* who had enviously sad eyes. "For the good, *gazdas*, for how much do we have of this life? Just a little bit!" And such wonder for that little bit!" He pressed Matronka, out of breath from the quick tempo of the dance, to his broad chest, and that's the way they stood, as though they were glued together in the middle of the wedding floor, until the first chords of yet one more indispensable wedding melody of this land was heard—of the grand festive circle dance, in Romanian—the "Hora Mare."[34]

After "The Hutsul Girl," frenzied, wild like a drunkard, and eternal, like a funeral lament, capable of shaking out your soul no less than an unclean force or demon[35] at midnight, the drawn out, slowed down, nearly sobbing melody of the "Hora Mare" is the same as a sudden stoppage of the heart, a jump to the other side of this world,

34   For a demonstration of the dance see: http://www.youtube.com/watch?v=RX8SZzcJd6o.

35   The *blud* is a type of unclean force in Carpathian folklore that when touched by someone leads that person to get lost and into danger. See the following for a more detailed explanation: http://storinka-m.kiev.ua/article.php?id=470. Many thanks to Olha Tytarenko for pointing this out.

or like an involuntary, blindfolded groping for the road to paradise and a voluntary exit from hell at the same time.

Nowhere can anyone anytime explain to you why this grand music of the deepest spiritual turmoil sounds like this. Maybe he, who was the first to place the melody he heard inside himself onto strings, knew everything that a sensitive person can experience in life, for he arranged those sounds into rhythm, as though into his craw: and he was pleased, and cried, or, maybe, just let out a sob after bathing in them... or he screamed as if he were in an icy stream's cleansing water.

Even with the most exact words and colors you will never be able to explain the strange inexpressible combination of the essence of the "Hora Mare," neither its ineluctable tragedy to a person who does not know what it is for a mountain person, the way you will never capture the sorrow in the silver fir eternally swayed by the wind at the peak of a cliff.

At first slow, as though unintentionally lazy, beseeched from all sides, and further—all the more dangerous and sharp, it suddenly covers over your head like a wave. The "Hora Mare" penetrates into a person unnoticeably—like a dream's delicious, sweet poison it enters into a woman lulled to sleep by caresses, and sneaks its way into an innocent soul the way a weasel sneaks under a cow's nipples, and painfully wounds like a dull knife that backbreakingly enters the body with a crack in the skin. Then that melody-thief swims in and pours in the veins unnoticeably—the way a person's own blood flows.

...First two steps to the left, then two to the right—and again left, and again right... after this you are allowed to turn around once, but don't have to... and then to the left... right...—and the two bodies of the groom and bride united into one swing as though they were a pendulum of a cumbersome wall clock, incapable of tearing away from its precisely designated spot or of changing the direction of its swinging. This merciless music-challenge in its slyness gives the dancer the first sign, and not even a sign. It shows the direction in which from now on these two will move only synchronically, only with the one who at this moment holds your sweaty palms in his hands; always and only together, not violating the tempo, without looking for another rhythm, just as in this strict and grand dance—not even a dance, but rather, a public but wordless oath for faithfulness till death or voluntary slavery together.

Then again two steps to the right... two left... to the vastly sorrowful wave of a violin or horn, with short-lived, momentary stops and breaks, as if before a gaping precipice... No, this isn't a wedding dance. This is a cruel, inhuman order of almighty forces about the impossibility of stepping out of line of the fate determined for you in advance....

Oh, the wedding choir is for one who hears it; it resounds like a warning, or, rather—a premature death knell, and perhaps, even a previous and somewhat unjust sentence for a human heart quivering from joy.

Maybe it would be better not to dance to this melody, sad like woman's fate, and eternally sharp, like the unavoidably raised ax of history over every person's head. Perhaps it's better to stand aside, leaning with your strained body against a fence or a tree, and just listen,

and think... think about everything—from the very beginning of the world, from Maria-Theresa, as they say in
these mountains, and till today, but by yourself. Perhaps,
it's better for you never to take that rhythm, eternally
given and immutable under any conditions, two steps to
the left, two to the right... For these movements, simultaneously slowed down by the two dancers in the middle of the emptied wedding floor, they are perhaps loftier
than the wedding oath itself, and stronger than the glue
of deceptive nighttime embraces. These rhythms force
their way through the pores under your skin itself. Even
through a thick-skinned person, they enter, like frostbite, like splinters, far beneath the heart, or maybe, the
violin drives them right into the very heart—and now
you will never voluntarily rid yourself of the subtle, nearly inaudible moan of the melody. You won't squeeze it
out of yourself, like the heart of a boil, you won't vomit it
out and drive it out—unless of course you die—and only
then will you jettison the charms of that music, like the
charms of a living fortuneteller.

Old timers say certain people hear the melody of the
"Hore Mare" just before death, for they say with such despairing sadness, with such unhurried steps—two—to
the left, two—to the right so as not to frighten or crush
a person with abruptness, death announces itself nearby....

...O, merciful Lord... Mykhailo and Matronka moved
that way on the empty wedding floor: two steps to the
left, two to the right, to the left — to the right... and then
just swayed, pressing their foreheads to each other; and,
it seemed, that these young newlywed orphans, want in

advance to outweigh or to push aside what awaits them in the future. The guests, especially the keen-eyed women, covered their traps with their palms, as if they also were striving to calm down the warning shouts about dangers that don't bypass anyone in life and, obviously, will not be emboldened to bypass this couple... For the newlyweds left the floor in such a strange and odd way for this village, that out of fear, one wanted to make the sign of the cross over them....

*

For a long time no one has ever been surprised by anyone in this village, because all manner of things had been seen in it.

Talk—they did talk a little about everyone, but—they weren't surprised. You think, no big deal: a lad brought from another village a small, invariably quiet and taciturn child, restless as a lizard, who will not say anything lame to anyone, and, in fact, not a word other than "Are you well-healthy?," "Lord help us!," "Be with God." He could, true, have taken one of his own village girls with a farmstead and a family, but as God already granted: a good fate also befits orphan outsiders. As long as she does not wag her tongue in the village like a windmill shaft, or cast spells—and the rest... let it be. Orphan to orphan—perhaps someday they'll be good farmstead owners.

That she is odd somehow and strange—maybe that's good: she'll keep her husband to herself and will keep herself to her own husband, and not to another man. Because things like this happen: a girl gets married, and before you know it, she becomes squint-eyed because she starts staring at other men's faces as if she doesn't have her own husband.

And this one stands there in the middle of the yard with palms folded, as though saying the "Our Father," and looks, keeps looking at Mykhailo—it's awful to see this from the side: any minute now, she'll fall before him as though before an icon, and will kiss his hand the way you kiss the hand of a priest.

And Mykhailo, without lifting up his head, chops wood, and now and again whistles so cheerfully through his two fingers, as though he's catching up with the devil after cocks crowing before dawn, or calling his love into the hay after a long time apart.

Matronka wipes the sweat from his forehead with her white apron, gives him some water to drink, and with her thin figure flows to her work. It's nothing but a wonder, and that's all there is to it! Is she out of her mind, or what?... They address each other with the formal "You."

Truth be told, this wouldn't be strange in their village if she would simply use the "You" like all the other women *gazdas*. But she speaks as if she's tasting that "You," chewing it, pressing it, rolling it between her teeth, like a sweet blackberry or dewberry. For just that single word many would rake her somewhere underneath a stack or in a roaring stream.

But men don't even smack their lips for Matronka like for other sluts or she-weasels. No one is able to say why. Either they're embarrassed, or afraid, or they pity such a tiny woman, whose bosom isn't very endowed and whom it would be easy to crush beneath you, let alone roll up in your embraces. And how has that pole of few words—Mykhailo—been dealing with her till now? Because she's a young woman, who, indeed, could live if not on her husband's palm, then, in fact, right in his bosom, only her hair would get in the way. Matronka had such a thick and long braid that she could wind it around her head three times, so that her bridesmaids looked for her wedding crown in her hair the way they would look for a poppy among bean plants.

Young women, enthusiasts for chatter, used to tell lies that Mykhailo, for sure, still had not approached her, because how would they really be so much in love with each other like it was before the wedding? And he still hadn't made her a child....

She most probably *refuses* him, and he, a simple man, can't beg his wife to let him come to her honeycomb. Already old but still foolish, he doesn't know how to approach such a thing; it's too bad that no one has taught the guy this ingenious work till now. But in the village there are those who could tell him how and from which side a man needs to catch his young wife so that she'd stick to him forever, as if she were glued to him. Or it might be another thing: Mykhailo may be unskilled in the art of *female sweets*, and that's why he's keeping his wife a virgin, so she doesn't age quicker, and he doesn't want to share his goods with anyone, and she, too, evidently, is not the kind who would give away her goods on the side. And, maybe, she herself doesn't know which free treasure she possesses.

In this or some other way, the polite female *gazdas* fibbed about Mykhailo and Matronka after Sunday mass while standing by the church walls for too long, and warming the smooth church pews with their hot backsides, and warming with their boneless tongues their mouths, tireless and black-gummed from lies.

*

...Matronka gave birth in broad daylight in the middle of March.

The village yet again in astonishment looked in the direction of their house: no one saw Matronka with a big belly, she didn't ask advice of anyone about giving birth, she didn't call a midwife, and the baby's crying—you can hear it all the way outside.

And how did Mykhailo do the delivery?

And how did he cut off the umbilical cord?

Why-why, the young village women couldn't forgive such ignorance. The time came to lash Matronka harder with their tongues.

Certain *gazda* maidens in the village weren't able to hide from the eyes of the villagers that they had become pregnant prematurely, though they pressed themselves in with belts and wore wide skirts with pleats. But a proper married woman, add to the fact she was such a small one, you wouldn't know the child was inside her, she tended to her garden nearly to the Feast of the Protectress[36]; every Sunday right on time she scurried to church; and she tied her shoes by herself to the last days.

But, the rascal, she didn't tell anyone! Maybe she didn't even tell Mykhailo either?!

---

36   October 1 according to the older Julian calendar, October 14 in the Gregorian. The feast day is also called the Intercession of the Blessed Virgin

"I've told you, dearie, you remember, mark my words, it won't end well… But who listened to me?! I said, look, good people, they're making the baby during the day, because they're keeping the house locked up during the summer day. Tell me which proper gazdas will lock their doors from other people for so long to make a single child? See, what I said happened?! Who-who, and You, my dearie, know well: any child born in the middle of the day was made in the middle of the day."

"Or isn't it all the same to you, Paraska, when someone makes children? One might think all ten of yours were made in the middle of the night and just in the winter!"

"No, you just think for yourself: the delivery finds the woman, and no one in the village knows! No one knows when that business was done, or by whom it was done.…"

"And you, what, my dear friend, wanted to light a candle for them, or show them when children are made?! They made it when the made it, when it worked for them. That's their business. And you should even be ashamed to think that the baby's not Mykhailo's."

"Say whatever you say, Kalynka, but they are good gazdas."

"They just avoid people."

"And why do they need people? People just make a mess in other people's lives. Maybe it's good for them without people."

"What do you mean why do they need people?! For control."

"Eh-h-h, my dear friend… It'd be nothing if a boy had been born. But it's a girl… and during the day no less, in the

---

Mary in the Western tradition.

afternoon... No one has seen that child, maybe she's a cripple... have you heard of such a thing that a man chops off a child's umbilical cord, when half the village here can chop one off? He didn't call Fulyachka... or the neighbor Marika, and Maria herself recently for the first time has had a child delivered, and knows all that business well... A woman birthing the first time is no heifer that's calving for the first time... and gazdas really need to watch, and here you have a tiny bit of a woman....

"As long as it's for the good, sweetie, everything... for the good... otherwise the child can possibly be mute."

"May your tongue break out in boils, Stefka, you're prophesizing such poppycock! Why would the child have to be mute when the mother and father speak?!"

"That's because a married woman can't conceal her bigness with seed. Pregnancy for a married gazda woman, that's not a disgrace. But Matronka hid her pregnancy right up to the birthing."

"You're saying stupid things, Paraska! Stupid! What, in front of the village she needed to bare her womb, so that a dumb shithead would know that they've finally made a child?!"

"Stupid—or not, but that's how my dead mother taught me, God grant her the heavenly kingdom."

*

...Did someone really cast an evil eye, or become envious, or simply did a time of suffering come to this house, who knows. But joy for Mykhailo and Matronka broke the way the string on Fitsyk's fiddle once broke right in the middle of playing "The Hutsul Girl" at their wedding, as though joy had never spent the night here.

...And it was like this.

The long spring roared away in winds and blossoms. The hills and valleys were taken by a sudden summer with frequent, short downpours, the untold splendor of the grasses and berries, and first and foremost—with protracted expectation of crops and litters of farm animals.

Matronka returned to her usual jobs—she unrecognizably blossomed after birthing, with an unwanted full bosom and a somewhat stifled, or, maybe, peaceful luster of her eyes.

Likewise –as before the child—she places a braid in a small rough circle around her head, she gets the child to fall asleep with her breast, carries out the sycamore maple cradle onto the porch, takes up her hoe, which is as small as she is—and goes to the garden. She rakes—strangely smiling to herself, closing her eyes for a moment, as though she's hiding something valuable in a place known only to her, then she suddenly looks back if anyone has seen her mysterious smile—and again takes to her hoe.

And toward evening she takes the child in her hands, rocks her, quietly singing, and moves closer to the gate. She peers for Mykhailo to come back from work. As far as work goes, he's not smart: till now he's been working for people. Chopping wood, setting out foundations, doing woodwork. In the village they often hire Mykhailo: without any worry they can even let him into their root cellars, and he won't tell a lie, and he hasn't got a sharp tongue, even when he is asked to, and he won't cheat, and he charges reasonably. And what great woodwork he did—no one could compete with him from the time Petro Tsiptsiar died—the woodworker and carpenter for ten villages all at the same time.

That summer Mykhailo was putting up fence stakes in the mountain pasture of the Cheremoshne caretaker Illya Dzhuryak, called Ilashka by the locals, so he would come home from the mountains just on Sunday. And his wife in the village would take care of the household. There wasn't too much to the household, but there was already a little: a cow, a pig, chickens, and three sheep. It's true, they didn't have much land besides what was near the house and in the garden, but Mykhailo girded himself with work like the rings on a barrel, intending to buy from Zaremba the miller a few acres of woods in Didkova Yama.[37] He already even gazed at that expensive green patch so that he sometimes saw it in his dreams.

But for the time being Matronka chased out all the cud-chewing animals before dawn to graze in the meadows above the Cheremosh River, and she has a peaceful mind till evening. Around sunset, she carried the cradle into the house, quickly ran to the river, herded in the livestock, milked them while singing, latched the door closed, and shut off the oil lamp in the house—she was hardly even seen.

But on a certain cloudy June evening, or actually, it was already even close to late night, Tanasiy Maksymiuk, who from time to time loved to grope around other peoples' yards to find his way to other peoples' young wives, noticed that the oil lamp in Mykhailo's house

---

37   Meaning "The Devil's Pit."

was flickering somehow strangely, as though it already had no intensity, and a child's cry wasn't a cry, and a sob not a sob—but a pitiful howling broke through outside even through the entryway door. Tanasiy didn't think for long—he just abruptly grabbed the door handle and shouted across the threshold of the dwelling:

"Are the *gazdas* at home?"

No one answered from inside the house: just beneath the window the cradle rocked with crying and distressingly sobbed and creaked in time.

"Matronka!" Tanasiy looked into the large living room and into the root cellar; and then with a poker rummaged through the house and porch; and then again looked at the entryway barrels and the benches by the house: "Hello to you, young woman, where are you, where the hell have you disappeared that your child faints from crying so much?!"

Tanasiy walked around the yard, illuminated by the moon that had grown white. The stable gaped wide open in the darkness; unusual cold, and emptiness; only the pigs were scurrying in the pen, flapping their ears, and snorting with their hungry snouts.

The neighbors, awakened from their sleep, shrugged their shoulders. Matronka stood bent over in the garden all day; then she went to Maria to sharpen her hoe and said she was going to herd in the livestock from the meadows, but she was a little late because of the hoeing. And then it was looking like rain, my poor head, and, you see, Maria, I'm still here, and you've already tucked the child into bed, and milked the cow, and went with that to her own house, and from then on Maria didn't see her, because she dragged herself to the house ahead of time....

The neighbors went with Tanasiy to search for Matronka in the meadows. They wandered about till the middle of the night. They found the sheep huddled together by the dam, but didn't find the woman or her cow.

What were they to do? They closed up the house. Maria took the child and put her in the cradle next to her boy. And then the village fell asleep as it did before this.

In the morning they told Mykhailo in the mountain valley.

That is how the misfortune began.

...Mykhailo ran from the mountain before midday. For some reason he took the child swollen from crying from Maria—and went to the Primar.[38] Yilashko was a good caretaker in Cheremoshne—he hadn't waited for Mykhailo to come from the mountain valley, but in the early morning had already sent two *gazdas* to the river to search. And just as Mykhailo appeared at the threshold, the caretaker advised him not to dawdle chatting and not to tarry with inquiries among the people, and just to go to the police station to file a report about his wife's disappearance. Yilashko already had filed a report, but it was necessary for Mykhailo to do this as well. There wasn't much hope, but there they know better what's going on in the village and even beyond its borders... the time was such, that it was necessary to dash wherever you could, while there was somewhere and someone to dash to....

Lieutenant Lupul, simultaneously the chief of the Cheremoshne police office and the border post, in Roma-

---

38 Romanian for mayor or village elder.

nian *posterunok*, silently listened to Mykhailo's report, for a long time twirled his sparse mustache beneath his nose, then sighed heavily, looking back at the wide open window, through which flies were scurrying, as though he were checking whether there was anyone by the wall, and said:

"Mihai, right now it's becoming really alarming here… soon a lot could change… but we'll search for your wife. The Primar sent his people, we'll give ours. We'll help."

Mykhailo ignored Lupul's uncertain words about his anxiety—it was as though he had gone mad from uncertainty. However he unexpectedly asked the lieutenant:

"Maybe the Poles have stolen her away to the other side?! She grazes the cow next to the river. And now they want a ransom?"

The chief of the gendarmerie sighed a second time:

"Mihai, soon it'll be a year already since there haven't been Poles on the other side. The Soviets are in charge now."

"I don't have any interest in that…," he half-heartedly interrupted.

"I have my own hernia…."

The lieutenant sighed a third time:

"They, on the other hand, do have a lot of interest in many things… But, I think, who-who, but they didn't abduct Matronka… there was no reason… Go home, *gazda*, and I'll lend you help with the search. God is good — we'll endure even this…," Lupul finished and for some reason patted Mykhailo on the shoulder.

*

For the second if not the third full day the male house-holds of Cheremoshne searched for Matronka—but the woman disappeared like a river Niavka[39] nymph. It was as if a living person fell into the earth without a trace. It was horrifying to think about such a thing happening in an inhabited place, and without anyone even noticing. Another time a chicken digs up a bed in a neighbor's garden and at the other end of the village the women *gazdas* argue about that trifle. And here such a thing... Yes, as though people on that day simultaneously went to sleep in the afternoon, and as though for the entire evening no one went to anyone else's house by way of the meadow either in secret or in full view, and as if no one that evening had gathered the sheep droppings along the riverbanks, or mowed the grass, or dragged firewood home from the meadow. Well, it's as though the entire village all at once went blind, or fell asleep in bed all at once even before sunset—and fell asleep as if they had died, and nothing in the world had concerned them other than deep sleep.

In the meantime in the meadow above the river not a single tiny bush or stone remained, under which grief-stricken Mykhailo didn't look after everyone, who had tried to help him find Matronka had looked before. He looked the way a crow searches every nook and cranny in a bone, pushed aside stones from their place and tossed brushwood prepared by someone before being carried out, for a long time probed the unoccupied river-

39   A mermaid-like evil being that inhabits rivers and seduces young men to their death. In Hutsul folklore they come from unbaptized girls or girls who suffer a violent death.

bank's surface, in case it would sink down or get soft, but he didn't find a single trace that would give even meager hope. Except for the trampled grass along the water itself and the tracks in the sand, which were heavy as though they had been forged, and evidently not a woman's. But no, not so. For Mykhailo not simply tracks were seen— but an entire trampled area of tracks right next to the water, as though here on the sand an entire army had marched or a large herd of livestock had huddled—as if crazed—not knowing where to come to rest, and then suddenly disappeared in the water. But Mykhailo found not a trace of the livestock, not a trace of a woman's foot, not even a tiny digit from her bast shoe, although Yurko Ohronnyk had given him his old binoculars from the Austrian war. And even when there was some kind of track, it stopped at the river....

*

In order to make it easier for you to imagine such an—almost improbable—picture of a mysterious momentary disappearance without a trace of not a mute, not a deaf woman, who additionally had lived locally for a long time, it would be good to in detail describe this locality, the landscapes, the location of the river, the surrounding villages and even the neighboring countries, in as much as the described events date back to June 1940 of the past millennium.

It's like this. On the two sides of the Cheremosh River, always murmuring and rushing no matter what season, shallow in spring and overflowing with water in the summer, between the hills and bald top mountains as though in the deep bosom of a woman, were nestled two mountain villages with the same name—Cheremoshne. If you looked at them from a bird's eye view or at least from the middle of the river, you could see that the villages reflected each other equally the same, the way a person's face is reflected in a mirror. From time immemorial the inhabitants of both Cheremoshne villages spoke nearly the same mother tongue, and the same way folded their hands to say the same "Our Father," on one and the same day celebrated Christmas and Easter, and even their dress was similar, and their oaths, and way of saying thanks. The people only greeted each other on the two sides of the river a little differently, that is nearly the entire difference.

But from time to time the land of their ancestors shifted from one country to another, like a weak-willed woman going into the arms of a more adept man, and because of that, from time to time and over many years, so many that they sometimes were chiseled into the centuries, the people under the twin hills were divided by a border that passed right along the middle of the river not subject to such changes.

On that day when the suddenly orphaned Mykhailo peeped under virtually every stone on the shoreline meadow, his Cheremoshne belonged to Romania, where King Mihai served as God and king for his subjects, and here, on the very border of Romania Mare,[40] in the village tucked into the mountains above the Cheremosh, the king's intermediaries—soldiers serving from the lo-

---

40   Greater Romania between World War I and II.

cal gendarmes headed by Lieutenant Lupul and the local landowners—were kings and gods.

When, who ruled, and for how long on the other side of the river, Mykhailo didn't know very well, but he knew precisely that in his memory the Polish lords, the *Pany*, along with their gendarmes and soldiers, maintained control over the people.

And since the past autumn, from the time the Poles, beaten by the Germans, withdrew from that land, more precisely, from September 17 in 1939, in Cheremoshne reflected as in a mirror across the river, the Soviets maintained control. They, to Mykhailo's surprise, in that year celebrated Christmas and Easter on the same day as on this side of the river.

…Mykhailo sits on the dam and, if not for the first time, looks with mute hostility, and, perhaps even with wrath to the other side of the water, where everything can be seen as though it was in the palm of his hand, and without binoculars. How much is there of that river? A frog can jump across from this side, especially when the river grows shallow, and the frog wants to scratch himself on a stone on the other side. In two particularly shallow places, there, where the stone is visible above the long-maned wave, striped border poles guard over the river, one of which the Soviets recently changed, but it was almost the same as during Polish rule, just more rickety, because it wasn't very well fastened. From time to time on both sides of the shores in unhurried steps the border guards with carbines measure the gravelly sand, silently glancing at one another across the water as they pass each other on duty.

Although, if you want to be totally and entirely precise, then on this Romanian, side, it's not so simple for those who want to reach the river at this spot from which Mykhailo glares like a wolf. Beyond the meadow, where the people's livestock grazes, along the steep, sheer precipice rises a really long dam—a fortification, constructed from good river stone from times when this side was still Austrian, partitioning off the meadows from the water. More precisely, it's not even like that. The dam doesn't so much partition off as it supports the steep cliff that sharply demarcates the village boundaries ten meters from the border.

Old folks say that the fortifications were built over an entire year, and then it took them a long time after that to fill in and even out the place between the cliff and the dam, where bushes now bend under the wind and livestock grazes. The dam beneath the cliff till now doubly protects the greater part of Cheremoshne from floods, whereas on the other side suddenly rising water often floods the gardens and even houses. But the opposite shore is more gently sloping, more of a plain, and therefore it's harder for the dam to keep the water away from it. But maybe, simply, there's no one to organize a good effort.

The Austrian dam on the Romanian side was not only old, well packed and reinforced, but for some reason had an unusual—arched form. From the other side of the river it was reminiscent of a somewhat deformed horseshoe that was bent a little from each side. They say that the *gazda* who organized its construction here was at one time not only a great landowner—a master of all trades, but also a bit of an oddball: he loved to do everything in a way that neither the locals nor people anywhere else would ever do. And they also say, he brought with him from the outside world a young German woman with weak lungs, so she had to walk above the water during the day in order to breathe in the moistness from the river as much as possible. The wife categorically refused to travel without her husband to warm waters for treatment. And so that it would be more cheerful for her to walk above the Cheremosh, that master thought up a small trick—he ordered the building of an arched dam, so that it seemed for his good Mrs. as if she were climbing up at first, like in the Alps, and then going down, up—down: this way, you see, the day passes more quickly, and it seems that you're wandering along other—distant lands.

Thus, from that time you could not only walk, but also even run along the wide crest of the dam.

But if you stand on this—highest—spot and suddenly look down at the river, then your head can start spinning, at least anyone's head that's not very healthy. And if you simply look this way—for the sake of interest, then below, right under the water one can see those kinds of shoreline bushes and stones like the ones here from above. Children would play and run downward along the dam, like tiny little suns after a rain along a rainbow, and then for entire days splash in the water. But their parents prefer to give their children a few beech switches on the butt than to let them swim around below the dam: they say, the place is cursed—and that's why it's unsafe.

Mykhailo sits on the crest of the dam, lowering down his legs that were worn out from walking, and looks at the other side. Cursed—or not cursed, the fact is true that the place is frightening. On more than one occasion children fell vertically headfirst, having gotten lost in contemplation of the noisy water; and livestock walked into the netherworld off the dam; and the border guards—*graniceri*—shot quite a few smugglers, *Schwarzivnyks*, as they call them locally; and they caught more than one drowning victim there. So the villagers strove to tend to the livestock in the meadow, enclosing the spot from the dam with a pen. And for bathing they went nearly to the end of the village, to the smooth, calmer water downstream closer to Zaremba's mill.

When the Poles ruled on the other side of the river, there were times that they looked at the smuggler-profiteers with a nod and a wink. Sometimes in the middle of the day they could find their way with their goods to the Romanian side. Whether the boatmen were in cahoots with the border guards, or sometimes unjustifiably took risks for the sake of profits, or the laws over there were a little bit loosey-goosey... But maybe because of the fact that Cheremoshne was nestled in the devil's bosom, the laws developed more loosey-goosey than anywhere else. However, on rare occasions it turned out that way for the resourceful profiteers. Or maybe, because of the fact that there was more to take across to the Romanian side from Poland than vice versa.

True, the Poles from time to time inflicted beatings on violators of the border peace during broad daylight, especially when the smugglers were from the Romanian side. They would send a poor guy caught in the middle of the river to their post. They'd beat him in the courtyard with beech sticks in their four hands. They'd take his goods. They'd detain him among the soldiers, force him to mow grass or toss down some hay, and then they'd send the beaten man home. And here the Romanian beech sticks play on him if not "The Hutsul Girl," then an "arkan"[41] all along his backside already black and blue from the Polish sticks.

After this for a certain very short time, the profiteering from both shores quiets down.

And again the border guards line up on both sides of the water nearly at the distance of an extended arm, they only don't talk to one another. But another day or two passes—and then from the other to this side a stone with aromatic Galician tobacco tied to it will whistle from a Polish guard on duty, and from this side—the *granicieri* will share dried plums in a bag, fastened to the top of a long and pliant fishing line or pole. And the boys in nearly exactly the same uniforms, if you look from this shore, will go in further along the river as though nothing happened, not reporting to the authorities this though minor, really strictly prohibited, violation.

…Mykhailo sits on the dam here and thinks that, in fact, he had lied to Lieutenant Lupul when he said he didn't have any interest in the formerly Polish, and just recently, Soviet riverbank. To tell the entire truth, he had no active interest, but Mykhailo does have eyes, and his eyes, thank God, for the time being are good, and he sees everything. He sees that from this last autumn the other side grew so quiet, as though there were daily funeral repasts for the recently departed. Or, it was as though peo-

41   A traditional Ukrainian step dance from the Carpathians. For a good example of one being performed see: http://www.youtube.com/watch?v=X5dMLSt36e0.

ple there suddenly gorged themselves on poppy stalks and fell into a sleep for a long time, like the forest uncle bears. Something's not right there... oy, not right, different from what it used to be before.

Say what you will, under Poland it was different. It used to happen that human shouts, shameless girls' squeals or satisfied young guys' whistles echoed from the cliff on that side to the one on this side, and especially on the days of church holidays or village triumphs. And the daytime or evening echo doubled the mixed voices, and they stood like a solitary pure bell in the valley cut by the water between the mountains. And whoever didn't know would not have said or even thought that the river, sinuous like a reptile, and green like feather grass, artificially marked with striped poles, makes that bell crack in half.

One day last winter when that side was still under the Poles, Mykhailo and Matronka were returning home from Christmas caroling late after midnight when they suddenly froze on the spot, having glanced at the other side of the choppy ice of the Cheremosh.

It was so nice there—that it was almost terrifying, the way, perhaps, a weightless soul is before the gates of heaven. White as though woolen snows lay from the top to the bottom as an immovable shroud, sewn just by the black peaks of the silver fir and beech forests, and tattered in patches of warm settlements above which a fragrant smoke curled. And tiny from afar, scattered among the silver, lustrous snows, these dark spots of houses shone now in cheerful Nativity play stars; and between the houses thin strings of carolers and Malanka[42] celebrators were visible, like laced shepherds' whips.

---

42   The church feast day of St. Melania, which is celebrated on January

And Mykhailo and Matronka leaned against each other so closely, that even through their coarse woolen coats you could hear the quickened beating of their hearts—because on that side a men's carol began to trumpet through a buck's horn, and from this side a women's carol rose abruptly in a violin, and suddenly the surrounding mountains shook from both sides with a single "Hey, God grant!" And Mykhailo wanted to fall face down into the snow on the silver hill from that side, where again the horn trumpeted invitingly, like a mature deer at mating time; because nothing else remained in the world besides the timorous, bird-like heart of Matronka in Mykhailo's hand, her hard, almost maidenly breast, and that Christmas horn first became alarming like the rumbling of flood water, then frenzied like a man next to a woman he finds desirable....

Sometimes after their daily chores, late in the evening, Mykhailo and Matronka went to the meadow, let their legs dangle from the dam, and listened either to themselves, or to the mountains' chilly breathing and the water's turbulent gurgling. They lean their heads against each other—and remain silent, they just toy with each other's hot fingers, and maybe just for a moment Matronka places her head onto her husband's knees—they listen... and keep listening.

And there, on the other side, some tipsy *gazda's* feet stagger—and he'll shout across the river to the same kind of tipsy guy, who's on his way back from Kapetuter's tavern; the whistle could be heard in both Cheremoshnes:

13, and corresponding to the Julian calendar New Year's Eve. In Ukrainian villages carolers and revelers would go from house to house singing New Year's carols and playing pranks.

"And what, *gazda*, are you going to yer girl this eve-nin'?"

"Why wouldn't I go?!"

"Does Mr. *Gazda* have a darling?"

"I do, may she stay healthy."

"May yours stay as healthy as mine, because I also have a darling; she's tasty as sour cream."

"Mr. Domnul, woulds you trade yer darlin' for mine? Mebbe mine is even tastier?"

"Mebbe I'd trade her just one time, but not more."

"So let's make a trade tonight."

"Go make the trade. Catch up with me."

"I'll go checks with the wife if she be lettin' me."

"Mine fer sure'll say: 'I'm not gonna let you.' Hows about yers—will she let you?"

"Mine might even let me, if it's not for a long time."

"Do you hear, *gazda*, how does yer girl give you a sign she can get away from her husband?"

"She hangs a mirror in the pear tree in the sun."

"And when there's no sun?"

"She hangs a scarecrow to chase away the crows."

And that's the way two tipsy *gazdas* call to each other across the river—so you can hear it in two villages. But no, it's not just two villages—but two countries apart where you can hear it.

On both sides the Romanian gendarmes and the Pol-ish soldiers scratch themselves and don't rush to drive away the *gazdas* willing to chat with each other. May-be they're thinking of their own lovers and girlfriends? But before they remember that one of the *gazdas* should speak in Polish, and the other in Romanian, the *gazdas*, look, have already disappeared among the houses like smoke. Either to their wives, or their lovers... all the same to their women...."

*

Since the time last fall when the Soviets arrived in Galicia, a few people from Mykhailo's village escaped to the other side. Why? For what reason? What came out of that escape—God only knows. Not a word was heard from them, not even a sign, as if the water had carried people off without a trace; except someone was gossiping about Kuryk that he was somewhere in prison on the other side ... But whether they were telling the truth, or lying, who knows? People like that—know how to lie better than to tell the truth.

Mykhailo doesn't understand this, because it doesn't concern household matters. He's just interested in his work and his household, but, God forgive, in the village Kuryk was so much the ringleader, that a little bit more— and he would have earned himself some prison time here. There are those kinds of people who bring trouble on their own heads. But that's their problem. Though, a whole bunch of Kuryk's children were left behind... And how could one run away from his own flesh and blood, and dump everything on the teeny tiniest wife like Mrs. Kuryk? And yet, something attracted the man there to Galicia, something stronger than his children and wife... Something attracted him. There Mykhailo's workbench and ax attracted him in a way that neither the tavern, nor carousing attracted him. Maybe someone wonders about him the way Mykhailo wondered about Kuryk and about those who disappeared with Kuryk to the other side.

…Mykhailo looks from the dam to the other side and feels that maybe for the first time in his life his heart was aching. And he senses a vague anxiety, as if right now the hawk that's hanging lifelessly over the nape of his neck as though over carrion is about to steal him, as though it's aiming right at his brow.

Mykhailo lifts himself up from the dam, takes a beech stick into his hands—and then makes his way across the meadow. For the umpteenth time he goes down to the water and from close up gazes onto the other side. From there a cold breeze wafts and the very same vague anxiety. And June is already passing… Soon one could cut wood in the forest for woodworking. You still can't do that now—it could be worm eaten. Wood for woodwork rots quickly.

*

…It was just beginning to dawn when Mykhailo heard a careful knock at the window. A somewhat perplexed Lieutenant Lupul with a carbine on his shoulder was standing on the porch. Mykhailo's heart grew faint.

Lupul started to speak in our language, which even more greatly surprised Mykhailo. The king's guards took good care of the villagers with forty lashes with a beech stick for violating the edict on speaking Romanian, *vorbiti romaneste*, so that more than one young woman on many occasions refused to be with her lover, so as not to have to show the slashes and bruises on her body, received for her tongue, which didn't want to speak a different language. So having heard his native language and not Romanian from the man who the entire time held a beech stick over the village, Mykhailo began to cough.

And Lupul in the meantime spoke quietly, almost in a whisper:

"Don't be afraid, domnul Mihai. Nothing's happened. I've just come to say that we are moving out of Cheremoshne. Tomorrow or the day after, the Soviets are going to be here. Different things can happen, Mihai. But there are good people everywhere, maybe they are among them. Don't tighten up, but go and tell them that your wife disappeared, and she's the mother of a nursing child. They may know something..." Lupul thought for another minute and added: "Difficult times are coming... Sure—make a report, but don't trust anyone absolutely. Look for your wife yourself."

Still warm from the bedding, for a long time Mykhailo looked from the porch at the cloud of the pre-dawn dust, whipped up by the rough bast shoes of a dozen well disciplined but poorly dressed of Lupul's soldiers, who slowly disappeared on the narrow village road in the direction of Beregomet, chased by roosters' crowing and dogs' yelping.

...And after a day, at midday the people reported that the authorities had changed in Cheremoshne....

Stamping around alone in his yard, Mykhailo went to the Jewish tavern to buy some gasoline, but, evidently, not in time. For the first time in his memory the tavern was closed. It's not for nothing people say: unhappy childhood, unhappy the rest of your life. Several times Mykhailo tugged on doors, peeked into the unusually shuttered windows, and with unhurried steps circled the yard. A frightful silence reigned in the always noisy household—you couldn't even see the household's triplet sons, bare-bellied in winter and in summer alike, but always in their yarmulkes—Yoska, David and Yakiv.

For some reason Mykhailo placed his ear to the tavern's entryway doors. For the longest time silence breathed heavily from there—you could only hear the mice in the attic pushing around nuts, and the wind rustled under the dried-out planks of the roof. And from farther behind the door a rustling could be heard, as though someone was shucking corncobs: then the door replied with the ingratiating, barely audible voice of Lazar Kapetuter—the owner of the tavern:

"Listen, mom... you should go back home... and don't be an eyesore with no need... Mom, I have gasoline, but these new hooligans with the stars and carbines have come for a long time, maybe even for so long that they'll live to see Sarah's and my death. And you're going to say to me that they have so much kerosene—up until my death?! I swear on my bald head that they'll also give us heat, and not just kerosene... so, for a while, mom, be without light. The day's long now. You don't need to have the light on. And there—as God grants... Mom, make children without light. The way Sarah and I make them. And if there are children—you don't need kerosene, because there are squabbles with children. And if we're gone—you don't need kerosene. On the other hand, the children remain.

Mykhailo sighed, not answering a word to Kapetuter behind the door, and headed off to Hershko's mill with an empty canister—to get the corn grits that Hershko had agreed to exchange for a new window. Mykhailo had carried the window over to the miller already two weeks ago, but he didn't manage to collect the grits.

White from old age or from the flour that had settled on him, the always obligingly smiling and unchangeably lively owner of the mill and the only village oil press sat now stock still by the mill's entrance. No, it wasn't like that: Hershko sat not at the entrance, but for some reason on a huge oval stone that was like an island in front of the entrance, dressed entirely in black, with his arms folded lifelessly on his knees. For a long time in silence he looked not so much at Mykhailo as through him, and then quietly said:

"To an honest person I wouldn't begrudge giving away my own … Take, my dear man Moishe, two, maybe even three sacks of grits and take them home, before I change my mind… The time might come when we, like mice, will be looking for a tiny bit of grain, and there won't be anyone who will give it, and then you'll remember good Hershko and will share your corn with him. Am I speaking truthfully, Moishe?"

"Such as a time has already come for me…," after being silent for a while, Mykhailo shrugged his shoulders and sat down on the mill's threshold..

"Oh, no, good man!" Hershko wagged his head as though only he knew something. "In your case, just your wife has disappeared. This is your only misfortune, though it's colossal. But your wife will be found. Mark my words. But today such times have come that the carriage goes—and doesn't see a person. It will run you over—

and you won't know what happened, that you no longer exist, neither your conscience, nor honor. The person is the same, but the carriage each time is different. Do you understand, Moishe? Each time different! But the person is the same."

"What are you saying, Hershko?"

"I don't know, but I'm telling the truth. No one said anything to me, but I sense it. My skin is on fire, because it senses it: that carriage that entered today in our life will not pass over the deaf, the blind, the Christian, or the Jew. Mark my words, good man… But now take your and my grits, think of it as ours, and hide it well, far away out of sight….

And I'll tell you that it can't be that not a single person has heard or seen any trace of your wife. It can't be! Those Judases always see and know what they shouldn't… But human nature is so bad, my good man…."

Mykhailo trod through the village as though not in his right mind. And there was no large sun. And in the gardens there was plenty of work, but the people somehow remained in their houses, so that there was no one to talk to. Except for near the bell tower some of the households gathered. But it was all the ones with whom Mykhailo didn't really want to chat. They lounged about more near Kuryk.

The bell tower's entrance for some reason was blocked off with a cart. Soldiers, who had come into the village, sat on the cart in worn out, faded brown military uniforms, in ratty boots, and some in bast shoes made from birch bark, with carbines over their shoulders. A dull conversation was going on between the households and the soldiers.

Vasylyna Makushkova stepped out from the chapel, which was next to the bell tower, wiping her eyes with the edge of her scarf, and behind her Dmytro Popovych, still a strong old man with an Opryshok's[43] hatchet in his right hand. They joined Mykhailo, who was turning the well crank in the old school yard. Popovych sat down on a round well casing, so low it was nearly all the way to the ground, filled his pipe bowl with tobacco and lit up the pipe, which looked so beaky, like Hafiya Berlova, the wedding cook from Cheremoshne. Vasylyna also lit up her pipe, drawing in sobs time after time.

"Why are you driveling, poor thing? " Mykhailo asked as gently as possible, giving her a cup of water. "Have you heard that my wife has disappeared? A nursing child has been left behind, and I'm not crying… crying won't help."

Vasylyna inhaled the fragrant smoke, held it in her nose, and then released it through her nostrils in swirling rings:

"I'm bawling, Misko my friend, for when I think what's awaiting us here, even a stone would start to cry. Take a look at this famine that has moved into our land! Tell me, my silver Misko, what good they can do for us and what good they can give us when they themselves are nearly bare-butted?! And take a look at their foot-cloths! At those shoes, woven from birch bark. You see, every day you walk in these fine pigskin shoes. And when you go out with people you have calfskin ones. Isn't that so?" Vasylyna asked and answered herself. "So think a bit in your head, what can they have when they go out on Sunday or a special occasion, if for the first time they

---

43   The *opryshky* were Carpathian freedom fighters, who revolted against Polish rule starting in the early 16th century until the early 20th.

stepped in like beggars among us, such polite *gazdas*??! Hard times be awaitin' for us, Misko. Mark my words.

Do you remember our landowner Floreskul? Oy, you don't remember, you was still very young then. Just remember our yardsman Yilashko, who could never be a landowner. My good man, did you ever see them around people dressed just anyhow with patches, and crumpled, likes they was dragged by dogs? Never! And you remember, how from across the river you could see the Polish lords from the other side, till doomsday, dolled up like they was goin' to a weddin'? They also was the authorities then. You don't remember that, 'cause you were still really young, but to this day I still really feel the number of beech switch swats I got from Floreskul for a tree chopped down in the wrong spot... The landowner could read and write, was tidy, and clean, but how awful and ferocious he was to people! What do you think, such a raggedy good-for-nothin' like this one, who spits in front of the bell tower, and no one knows where he had his belly button snipped, can he be much better or kinder than the Romanian gendarme or the educated landowner? Would you be able to think that someone from the police office could spit in front of a church?! And you ask why I'm sobbing... Oy, my heart feels it, this won't pass over us."

Dmytro Popovych listened to Vasylyna in silence, with his ax tapping the gravel around the round, wood-enclosed, tin-roofed well and then let out smoke through his white mustache, twirled up on each side:

"You see, Misko, Vasylyna is telling the truth: nothin' good will come of it."

"You think so?" Mykhailo asked again for the sake of form.

"And you take a look at their officers scurrying through the village as though they're mad. In the Austrian war I wasn't a senior officer, I was just a senior soldier wherever they sent me. And after the war I served two more years in the army. And I can tell you no worse than an intelligent man how and what will be. So I'll say to you, Misko, even when I was a soldier, it wasn't for nothin' that I ran around and churned up the dust along the road, scaring out the dogs, the way those now are poking about from the bell tower to the gendermie, as though they're mistaken in the head. You see, our poor Annytsia, who lost her mind, and she walks about the village calmly, even when it smacks her in the head. What of it if she flails her arms around—that's nothing. But she doesn't cause people to fear her. But these somehow are so agitated. Nervous people can't calm down other people."

Mykhailo looked from the well to the bell tower—and felt a hotness pouring out from inside from the fact that everything was the way that the former Austrian soldier Popovych said:

"Tell me, is something burning or in flames, why are they rushing around just gettin' on people's nerves? When the new authorities, Misko, come to the people to mess with their heads, they should be calm, peaceful, so's as to calm down the people, if they want things to be good where they are coming. But this way—all over the place… We've seen this more than once before.

I think like this… They've come—well, that's good, gather the people together. Explain what's what.

Because before they arrived, their reputation precedes them. Some famine was over there in Ukraine, but did they say anything about that? They didn't. People from Galicia passed that along, that so many farmstead owners from there were taken away, and not even the family knows where they are and what they're doin'. Who's going to treat them well? If they don't tell the whole truth— then there's something going on there. And you look, what kind of mess is happenin' in the world. A conflagration. And here they're stokin' you a fire inside people, so's you don't know what you have to extinguish it with.

So Vasylyna's tellin' the truth, don't expect anything good, just look for your wife, because she's your greatest friend, and no one else in this world is more of a friend to a man."

"Why bother with them when I have my own worries?" Mykhailo asked diffidently, looking first at the bell tower, then at Vasylyna and Popovych.

"Eh-h-h, I'm not so sure... You think that you'll get by without them, but they won't get by without you for sure. For sure I'm telling you, Mykhailo! And don't even think about it!"

And then Mykhailo doffed his hat before both of them and set off wandering his way home along the empty street.

A Romanian gendarmerie was located across from the bell tower until quite recently. Now the very same soldiers who previously had blocked off the entrance to the bell tower were sitting on its porch, and kept spitting pumpkin seeds onto the ground. They were chatting with each other loudly, so loudly that Mykhailo even recognized several words. But their language was a little bit different… and Mykhailo didn't go up to them to make a report. His wife is his worry. He just returned to Maria's house for the child.

"You should, silver Mykhailo sweetie, somehow calm down the child. You should give her a rag soaked in poppy seeds—she'd at least sleep. 'Cause for two full days the poor girl is crying without a teat—her hair's standing on end. And she can get a hernia from crying."

"I give the child cornmeal and Maria brings milk. And the child is more at Maria's, God grant her health. I'm not going to give her crushed poppy seeds. The child is supposed to be smart. We'll find Matronka—she'll feed the child."

"…I'm going to say something to you, kind Mykhailo sweetie, but don't takes it wrong for me sayin' it, 'cause it's the holy truth, may lightning strike me if I'm tellin' a lie. I once said to your gazda: don't feed the child, mistress, just with your breast, anything could happen. Grind up some green beans, taters, and feed her—she'll be healthier. But no—she just kept feeding her with breast milk. That's youthful reasoning for you! Youth is foolish! And she doesn't want to listen to an elder."

"Matronka had a lot of milk, and she did good giving it to the child. Life is a long-time thing. Who knows what a child will be fed with in this life? And she'll grow healthier from breast milk."

"Yes that's so, golden Mykhailo sweetie, but you see what's happened… And if only your own mistress would have listened to other mistresses, then, maybe, she would have been nicer to you…."

128

*

...Matronka was found on the third day. More precisely, on the third day Mykhailo found her there... where for three days he had searched for her, like a fish under rocks: in the meadow.

Regarding that, people said something like she fell from the dam at night and lay unconscious this entire time there in a hole, a place where the village population dumped useless junk in wheelbarrows.

In truth, the hole was pretty big. But even more truthfully, hardly anybody believed that Mykhailo didn't rummage his way through the hole to the very bottom when he was looking for Matronka himself. And why in the devil's name would anyone crawl onto the dam when the cows graze closer to the rocky shore, in the meadow, and the dam goes behind the meadow, and in addition is fenced off from the pasture ground with wire and pole fences?

Or maybe some kind of lover had arranged a meeting with her right above the water, or with what kind of unclean force did she consort with that carried her off in the evening to the dam, and add to that when her husband wasn't home. Matronka is a reserved woman. And what in damnation dragged her there—only she herself knows.

Even if none of the men had looked into the trash hole, then Mykhailo already had done that for sure....

But what doesn't happen in the world. His wife was found, but a cow, you see, disappeared without a trace. How can such a thing happen? If a cow had been smashed to pieces from falling, the dead cow would have been found. If the water had taken it—then somewhere from another village they would have let us know that a dead cow had floated there. And so there is no cow as if there had never been any cow. It's a miracle—and *gata*.[44]

That's what people related word for word to each another. And how it happened in truth—God only knows. There were no witnesses. The village calmed down quickly: each has his own misfortune in his own house. And then add the fact that new authorities promenade through the village and make the blood in your veins turn cold.

And it's a good thing that the woman was found: the priest's wife won't get money for another woollen blanket, and there will be space for one more coffin in the graveyard.

"...I don't want to commit a sin, my dear friend, but let's admit the fact that something unclean might be involved with that Matronka... It's possible she's a witch, dearie, though from her appearance she looks very gentle and hard working... Maybe she turned from a person into a witch that night, and then back into a woman, and someone caught her in the act; and then you know, God forbid someone from seeing a witch turn into a person. ... And maybe, that's why all this happened... maybe, during the night she clambered somewhere through the forest onto one of their witches' gatherings. We don't know who her mother and father were. Maybe, they were from unclean blood? If you look at her in the evening from behind—then maybe you'll see just her intestines and innards."

---

44   "That's it" in Romanian.

"Probably, that's why Mykhailo's the way he is, he's like a man possessed. Remember, Ivan from Kinashka was benumbed the same way. But a chimney flue opening hit him with plum tree firewood. And there's nothing worse on your head like being struck by plum tree firewood. It's good that his wife found Ivan. And if his wife hadn't returned by morning from that there lover of hers, then she would have lost her husband and lover. Because that's the way it is. A lover loves a young wife only if she has a husband. And when a lover doesn't have that, he just looks somewhere else.

"What can I say to you, Payutka... You've talked a lot here—three water-skins full and two sacks full of astonishing stuff. You just didn't know where the lie was, and where the truth. I already forgot where you started... You're telling the truth, anything can be. But she doesn't looks like a witch. Doesn't looks like one—and fertig.[45] May I not stay healthy if I'm wrong. I'd stake my head on it she's not a witch. Witches, they always have a red face, but she has one that looks like it's greased with sour cream on top of wax. She's some kind of anemic, and not a witch..."

...Mykhailo didn't allow anyone, not even the village healer, to examine his wife: Matronka was bruised all over. Not as though she had fallen from a height, but rather as if someone had beaten her with beech switches or whips all over her body, especially over her back and legs: large bruises and clotted blood spread over her *body* like fallen rotting fruit in the garden. Her fingers looked like they had been pressed by pliers or struck with stones. Her breasts were swollen from an excess of long unexpressed and clogged breast milk, and then a fever hit her and lasted a week, and then the milk in her

---

45   From the German meaning "that's it."

breasts completely dried up—and Mykhailo began to wean the child on cow's milk and everything else edible.

For a long time Matronka lay immobile on the bed by the window and was mute. She looked first at the windowpane, then at the ceiling, from time to time sighed audibly, silently crossed herself and again kept silent. Maybe she talked more with Mykhailo, but no one heard it. And whoever came to see Matronka found one and the same picture: from time to time his wife sighing on the bed, propped on all sides by pillows, with tips of her fingers bent to make a sign of the cross and Mykhailo, silent, with the child in his arms.

"What it is dearie, when a man doesn't know another woman, then he's quick to kiss his wife's ass! You just look at our Mykhailo! The man completely lost his head after Matronka disappeared. He abandoned his work, doesn't show himself in public; he just minds his own business with his wife and child, as though nobody before has been in any distress. Look too—a man will perish because of that kind of lover."

"Hey to you, dearie, something so stupid has come into your head! It's true that sweetheart has been the ruin of more than one man, but she isn't just a whore, but a married woman! But what would you want, when she's so weak, poor orph-a-a-an? Did she maybe lose her way that night, or does God know what happened? You see yourself, both are suffering—and they aren't showing their misfortune to people."

"What's there to bear to people? If something good would … but here you have just a total headache…."

"Eh-h-h… old people used to say: you can't really love as much as these two loved each other, not taking people

into consideration... Because no one, not even God, likes it when a person lives—and just takes pleasure. A person, while they're on the earth, must suffer. And in heaven they will take pleasure."

"Until you'll be going to heaven—there other people can snatch away all the joy. So you need to take pleasure while you're alive. But what I want to say to you... have these two done anything bad to people?! And they're very young... they have time to eat heartily of all kinds of misfortune. They've been punished too early, too early. Are they paying for someone else's sins? You know how it is... sin follows after a person from the seventh generation. So don't think, dearie, that all this is so simple."

"A person when he's happy is rich. He doesn't see others. He thinks that he's grabbed God by the beard. When in fact it's God who keeps him on His hook... And a person, moreover, who's happy, needs to see everyone. And everyone must see him. Then all are equal. But these two wanted to be superior."

"Though it's foolish, dearie, you say, this is worldly wisdom... And to be perfectly honest, then, for that matter, these two didn't want anything... except they wanted to be separate from everything. And it doesn't work out like that."

*

...Mykhailo tended to Matronka for the summer, fall and all winter.

He fed her with warm milk and honey,
    warmed her with the skins of suckling puppies,
    he steamed her in infusions of arnica and valerian,

rubbed her with badger fat,
and wrapped her in pork casings.

And the fact that he didn't let her do any work goes without saying.

So that people bothered them less with peeking and questioning, he even changed the tattered picket fence into a solid one around the pen, which gave rise to more dissatisfaction among the young women, who loved to inspect other people's farmsteads, in a way they didn't always love to inspect their own cast iron pots.

Covered in a white scarf, Matronka sat down on a block of firewood in the middle of the yard, she crossed her palms as though saying the "Our Father," looked at Mykhailo, who was cutting out boards or planing stock for woodworking, and cried quietly. She didn't sob and didn't snivel, didn't wipe away her tears and didn't blot them—just large tears rolled along her face and wouldn't stop, as though they wanted to swim along her sour cream face all the way to the very sea.

"Does your head ache, Matronka?" Mykhailo quietly asked, putting his palm to her forehead.

"No. Why are you asking?"

"Nothing."

"Then why are you crying?"

Matronka sighed, then wiped her tears with the corner of her scarf—and so serenely looked into Mykhailo's eyes, as if it were just before her wedding. And then she suddenly remembered and asked:

"Where is my miracle?"

The tiny—like a poppy seed—miracle in a bright woven dress, in the same kind of material as Matronka's scarf, quickly moved her chubby little legs in her small bast shoes, trying to touch a rooster with a little thin switch. Reaching the red comb of the surprisingly submissive bird, the miracle child stopped, smiled to both of them at the same time—and with a shriek ran, stumbling, to her mother. Matronka pressed the child to her bosom so tightly, as though someone at that moment was trying to take her away, and kissed her round little head and again began to cry.

Mykhailo left his work, took his wife and child into the house, put her on the bed, leaned over her as it used to be during dinner, his forehead pressed against her forehead, and asked again:

"Tell me, Matronka, why are you crying? What are you keeping secret from me?"

"Beforehand, Mykhailo sweetie pie, I'm crying... beforehand my heart is crying...."

"Matronka, my dead mother once told me: you must not grovel beforehand, because you're summoning misfortune to yourself."

"You don't need to summon misfortune. Misfortune has long been all around us. It's only unseen—like death...," Matronka somehow spoke strangely and turned to the wall.

*

...Nearly a year passed in such torment. Weakness little by little let go. But no one saw the happiness and liveliness anymore that once was in Matrona's eyes and hands.

Not even Mykhailo saw it....

And in Cheremoshne things stirred like under a gypsy girl's skirt.

The new authorities shuttered Kapetuter's tavern with crisscrossed boards, and how the Kapetuters managed to live now, no one knew, but they lived worse now than they used to before. And instead of a tavern in the two rooms of the former Floreskul estate, the Soviets opened up a cooperative, and the rest of the property they distributed: a room to a medical assistant, a room for a workshop to repair various domestic utensils, one to the shoemaker, two to the dairy. The formerly spotless estate became so crowded that now there was total disorder.

Perhaps from that misfortune right on Christian Easter Sunday Sarah gave Kapetuter yet one more boy, and now the Kapetuters could boast of four sons. But it's not very good even for a Christian to give birth to children on Easter Sunday, not to speak of a Jew. Although, as they say one born in the light of Christ's resurrection will remain happy his entire life, but at the cost of the death of someone in the family. The Kapetuters were devout Jews, but they also believed in Christian signs, and now Sarah, fidgeting with the smallest one, Samuel, at her breast, kept secret from her husband that she worried about who in the family had to die before their time.

Now in charge of Hershko's mill was the biggest and loudest village slacker—Lesko Onufriychuk—at whose place the picket fence near the house had been propped up all over with patchwork since the dawn of the world's and sun's creation. You would not find another man who would know how to fool people's heads wagging his empty and boneless tongue the way Lesko did… True, no one

136

needs a man who works wagging his tongue at the mill, but the authorities know better.

And Hershko now from time to time was there to help the new miller, who each time asked from which side you needed to approach the wheel. The former owner all the more often sat himself down on the stone in front of the mill and took a *drymba* to his lips, which surprised those who came to the mill when they needed to. "It's better to play the *drymba* than to speak what's on your mind …," Hershko on more than one occasion justified himself, but this sounded overly sad for the always cheerful nature of the elderly Jew, from whom, additionally, they took away even his oil press—and now its entrance also was covered up with crisscrossed boards like Kapetuter's tavern. But people squeezed out oil anyhow and anywhere they could.

They made a village reading room in the former Romanian school, but no one now went there to read. But whoever wanted to, secretly kept going to the former "Prosvita" (Enlightenment) building, which was banned before by the Romanians, just as it is now by the Soviets. And they drove people to the reading room by force, in order to hear what was happening in the world from the lips of a new lecturer each time. And also, off and on they would show a movie, but you didn't have to call them to the movie more than once—people came themselves, they even ran, to look at people like them who moved along the white linen screen as if they were alive. Some of the women swooned time after time, the men twirled the tips of their mustaches, but the majority mostly remained silent. Nothing good was happening in the world. Nearby on the side in Poland war was ablaze. And old guys from before the flood reported in a whisper that their dreams foretell an impending red sky somewhere near here, maybe even in their village.

And they moved the school into the spacious building of Cheremoshne's priest, cramming his large family into the former store of Yuz Rozenfeld, who escaped together with the Romanians, not taking with him even the dirt under his fingernails.[46] The goods were taken from Rozenfeld's store in the middle of the night without any witnesses, and the priest's belongings were transported in broad daylight by four carts in two trips.

And at one moment Mykhailo realized that in his village it was slowly becoming as quiet as Cheremoshne on the other side of the river, though there wasn't an increase in corpses in the village, and typhus didn't mow down people. As before, people celebrated weddings, patron saint church festivals, and baptisms, but their festivities became somewhat shorter and depressed, and the village—sad and taciturn, like a woman who cries herself out half a year after her husband's death.

One late June night someone banged at full strength at Mykhailo's door. Paraska Danyliuk, the closest neighbor of the Kuryks, was standing on the porch out of breath with a linen bag in her hands.

She brusquely pushed away Mykhailo from the door and, uninvited, ran into the house. Matronka at that moment was putting away her evening sewing into a basket.

"Dearie Matronka, I see that you want to embroider a new shirt before the Feast of the Blessed Virgin, but the

---

46   An idiomatic saying in Ukrainian meaning "a tiny crumb." It's literally the "dark blue" under the fingernails in the original.

day of the Blessed Virgin is still far away, so just put that aside and go with me right now; I won't forget you forever if you do. You're a good woman. You won't tell anyone, and it'll be of use to you. You could use some new household goods and clothes. And I'll make myself look smart. Because I'll get some new clothes for church. And I can't hold a needle in my hands like you do, and my eyes aren't very good either."

"Hey, no good will come out of it, woman," Mykhailo stopped her discontentedly. "Stand hereby and tell us properly what's the matter with you, why you is like that, as if a stake got shoved up your behind."

Mykhailo didn't like Mrs. Danyliuk, because he knew without other wagging tongues that Paraska was fond of other people's things, and she had sharp eyes, but not for a needle and thread or for the spinning wheel.

"Golden Mykhailo, let Matronka help me. I can't lose what's mine. Kuryk once made such a hullabaloo in my house that till now I'm left without my husband. And till now the marks from the gendarme's beech switches and belts haven't disappeared from my back. I then lost my child because of Kuryk, may lightning strike him still in the womb, as he's ruined more than one person's life here! But God is good. He sees everything. God beats us not with a beech switch and not with a rolling pin, and not on your butt, and not on your back.

"Mrs. Danyliuk, stand up!" Mykhailo shouted, which startled the baby sleeping on the bed. "What's happened to you—has your tongue been broken, what's wrong with you that you can't speak sensibly?! What Kuryk? Where's Kuryk? It's been nearly two years that the children have been crying for him!"

And here Paraska to his surprise quietly sat down on the bench near the wall, grabbed a cup of milk from the table and in a gulp drank it down, and now slowly said:

"The Kuryks have come to no good! Everyone's come to no good. The girls at a marrying age, no plot of land—not even a little piece, not a single *falcha*,[47] and they sewed flags and stirred up the people. What, haven't you seen who ran out with the flags, sewn in blue and yellow, all the way to Khorova to meet these bandits who have been in charge in the village for a year? The Romanians' tracks haven't even worn away, and the Kuryk girls for Easter got dressed up in embroidered skirts and tied Canadian scarves on their heads, like bridesmaids, and they were carried off with those flags, jumping right to the front of the line, may misfortune take them. And what did they get from it? What? Tell me, golden Mykhailo sweetie? Tell me, silver Matronka?! Maybe the Russkies paid them back with land? Or with livestock? Maybe, they sent their young children to some there highfalutin' school that opened up in Vyzhnytsya? Did golden dust from the king's throne fall on them? What, tell me, besides the people's disgrace have the Kuryks known this year?!"

"Why would you care about those Kuryks, Paraska...," Matronka finally began to speak. "To each his own. Their father was like this, and he taught the children this way. The children took after their father. If something's not the way they wanted it to be... then who can know? You think one thing—something else happens."

"Your head has to think, Matronka, and not your backside. But if Kuryk wanted to play politics, then why

47   A measure of tillable land a little less than three acres. Many thanks to Olha Tytarenko for pointing this out.

140

did he drag in my *gazda*? And Petryshyn's Slavko? And Dzhodz? Where are they now, I ask? When they went to the other side to find Russky happiness—they disappeared, disappear, misfortune, in the muck! Do you think they found something there? Maybe a bump on the head. And the children are now suffering as a result of their stupid father.

"And what about the children? Petro serves as the Kuryks' errand boy with the Soviet *prymar*. The eldest Marika is washing floors in the school. You see, they gave her work." Matronka defended her not so much out of wanting to, as much as wishing to get Paraska out of the house quicker.

"Wake up, Matronka," Mrs. Danyliuk threw up her hands, "Although you fell from the dam, you're not stupid and not a witch like people say. What's not clear here? They're taking the Kuryks from the village! They're moving them out this second. Just look, they're packing them up right now onto carts.

Why did I come to you? Before dark I was about to go to Mrs. Kuryk to argue about their goat that chewed up the plum tree in my garden and very nearly hung itself in the tree, and I would have been at fault for the goat's death. But here this happens... I look from the walnut trees, there are military people scurrying around in front of the Kuryks' gate, like a cow before giving birth, and in the pen there are also military people, and they're all shouting and rushing. And I stood in the shadow of a mulberry tree behind the stable and heard everything. They told everyone to pack up. To take warm things and nothing else. They had to be ready in an hour. And on the other two carts on the road the wife of Petryshyn's Slavko with her children and mother-in-law were already packed and crying, and Dzhodz's *gazda* wife was sobbing with her children.

It took a long time for the Kuryks to get ready, so one of them hit Petro so hard with his carbine in the shoulder—that he fell over by the threshold. Maybe they are already gone. Because they said not to speak, not to make noise, and just quietly prepare, and if they would prepare quietly, then they said that they'd let 'em go to the cemetery to their relatives to pay them a visit before the road. And say farewell. At night. Do you understand what's happening? They're taking them like thieves. But the Romanians would have led the thief out before the people in advance, and would have given them a good beating, and then would have taken them to jail. But the Kuryks didn't steal anything; they just served them faithfully. They did stir up the people—but a word doesn't hurt if you carry a head on your shoulders and not a pot. But that's it. Only the dust rose after the Kuryks. And I thought, maybe I sinfully thought, but there must be justice in the world: haven't I suffered a great deal because of these Kuryks? Then why do strange people have to take their household goods? Look right now, soon a lie will spread through the village, that they took the entire family, then there will be enough of those willin' to scrounge around in their root cellars, though they were empty, but all the same, somethin' was left, because they didn't let them take anything on the road.

What, can't I take those embroidered Easter blouses or tasseled Canadian scarves? They took my husband from me, and they called me a whore for no reason, because (according to their logic), the minute a man's foot steps into my house that makes me a whore, you see. Whoever takes from someone else, God gives the same to them. Don't you think, golden sweet Mykhailo, and you, silver Matronka… I'm not joyful that they took away the Kuryk family, but truth must sometimes rule among people. And we don't know where they've been taken to. Maybe they want to pay them back for those flags that the Kuryks' children carried all the way to Khorova, but in such a way that no one in the village sees or knows, and wouldn't be envious?! Well what—they're so wise, and I'm stupider?

Tomorrow other *gazdas* will come—and all the same they'll take away their goods. And what, I'm going to have good things go to waste? Come with me, Matronka, let her, Mykhailo sweetheart, because it's horrifying for me to go into Kuryk's empty house. There, maybe the polenta from yesterday's dinner is still warm....

*

…And in a week the dreams of Cheremoshne's gray beards came true, those who in their youth, obviously, had their fill of sniffing gunpowder in battle so well that they smelled from afar the rising of the most recent powder in a world powder horn.

Several days after the secret departure of ten families from Cheremoshne to parts unknown, a new war happened in the world.

You wouldn't say that something extraordinary happened in the village.

The new, still short-lived authorities disappeared without saying "farewell" and without a "thank you," for at least the fact that the people of Cheremoshne tolerated them for an entire year. For a certain amount of time in all the localities and on that side of the river complete anarchy reigned, so that the old men went to ask their former caretaker Yilashko to once again bring order to the village. Some moved with their entire families to the mountains where just the devil says "good night"—far away from what inevitably must come with the war.

And Cheremoshne's Jews after an imposed interruption returned to their former Geschäft[48]: Kapetuter opened up his tavern again, Hershko—both the mill and a tavern.

The rest of the Jews followed their lead....

*

...Hard times came... on Sunday, Tanasiy Maksymiuk, who had shrunken to the size of a child, smoked his pipe while sitting on a bench by the wall of Maria's house.

The sun shone brightly.

After the church service the church bell dully clanged in the distance.

Two large hawks, seeking their prey, hung above Mykhailo's house that was next to Maria's.

And a dog also yelped on the road. And chickens bathed in the roadside dust.

"Nowadays aren't for life or for joy, really just for thinking and death...," Tanasiy wagged his head. "Look,

---

48   "Business" in German. It's spelled in Ukrainian transliteration in the original.

even the hawks don't move away from Mykhailo's household... What kind of evil place this is! I said that once
to Mykhailo—don't extend the thatched roof from behind, put in a veranda. If you want to, widen the house,
or make a storehouse on the side, but don't add to the
thatched roof from behind. That won't end up well. And
look, Maria, from the time he extended on to the old
house, their misfortune began. And here even without
that hard times have come.

"And when were they not hard?" Maria asked while
she was mixing dough for dumplings in the summer
kitchen.

"They were, when we weren't here. Then when we
were in the womb."

"Eh-h-h, I don't know about that...," Maria looked at
Tanasiy, wiping the sweat from her forehead and fixing
her young bosom. "Even in the womb, *gazda*, it's hard,
because we're in captivity there. And it's really dark. So,
Tanasiy, the times—are the times they are, and fate—is
fate. Misfortune doesn't depend on time... Maybe, the
extended thatched roof is to blame, and maybe, fate is
written this way for our Mykhailo... But, look, they love
each other dearly, as if they had just gotten married yesterday, and live quietly, like mice in a hole in a tree. And
everyone has misfortune, just not in the same way."

"There is no denying the truth in what you are saying, Maria. If everyone chased out his misfortune to the
village gate and examined it well, then he would snatch
his own right back, because it's even worse for others...."

"You don't really understand this, because a dame
has no idea what the war's about and doesn't know squat

145

about military matters. But look, Maria: the Romanians gathered up men for the slaughterhouse of war—and who knows how many of them will return, or have crows already scattered their bones? And if someone returns then what will be further? And listen, good woman, it means something that no one heard or saw that the Romanians have cleared out now from the village under German orders, as once the Russkies did?! They were here over twenty years, and the Germans in a single day cleaned them out like ashes from the storehouse. It's not without reason now that instead of the Romanians the Hungarians are trudging through the village and leading our girls astray. It's obvious the Germans don't really trust the Romanians when they want to maintain defenses with those vile Hungarians. During those days Onufriy Matios from Okolena would come down and say that they dug up trenches all over Okolena and were making ready a second line at Siruk. It's apparent there will be a great slaughterhouse here tomorrow if not today... Something's changed at the front because you hear the cannons approaching. And once the canons are shooting already somewhere from near Berehomet, then it means the Germans have decided to retreat. And once the Germans retreat—the front will shift, they can evacuate the village. That's the way the Germans do it... I'm not sleeping at night, I feel the earth move, and think to myself in my head. I think about everything, Maria....

You're still young, and don't know anything of life, not even as much as the dirt under your fingernail, you don't know anything. And you don't need to know. Give birth to your children while you can and you have someone with whom to do it. Because they'll sweep away all the menfolk—there won't be anyone left to make a baby. So don't avoid someone else's husband, if he asks, because such a time might come that yours might not be... And just in case carry off some of your household stuff somewheres over there in the forest and bury it, because if you need to evacuate, you won't be able to take even a pinch of salt, it can happen like that... I'm telling you for certain, hard times have come—and there will be even harder ones... In my lifetime I've seen a lot, but not even I have seen this. And what happens further with the people?...."

*

...And before it was like this, that in Cheremoshne at the beginning of the war, a small German detachment entered and billeted among the people. They put the German field kitchen in the garden of the Cheremoshne caretaker Yilashka, and in the former Soviet military command office now there was also a German military post.

The Krauts in the village conducted themselves peacefully. They just went to all the houses and took the fowl and pigs for butchering, but the Germans didn't come to anyone for chickens two times, which gave rise to silent approval. And they didn't particularly bother the people. They passed out to the children long candies in shiny wrappers never seen before in Cheremoshne and some kind of strange fruits that were apple-shaped.

On the second day after their arrival, the Germans through their envoys called the entire village to the church for an open meeting. A German officer in boots waxed to a luster, a tall black cap with a tall cockade and a well pressed black full dress uniform with an emblem on his sleeve that resembled the design on *pysanky* Easter eggs decorated in Cheremoshne—with two clamps crisscrossing each other and curved in different directions. He spoke in brief sentences, and Tanasiy Maksymiuk translated the German conversation into words the people could understand. He had spoken German since the Austrian war.

The German said that great Germany and the great fuehrer Adolph Hitler had begun the war with the Bolsheviks for the sake of freeing the occupied people from fear and outrages; he said not to fear the war, but to listen to the new authorities, and to forever forget those who caused people harm over the course of the last year.

The new administration will open a school in the village.

The priest will do a church service every Sunday.

The right will be returned to people once a week to legally have contact with their families from the other side of the river, where German authorities were also in charge, as they will soon be in charge over all of Europe.

A German doctor will come to the village and treat all kinds of infections that the Bolsheviks propagated and encouraged.

The German also asked to remember those with silence, whom harm touched the most, and from a sheet of paper read the names of ten Cheremoshne *gazda* men, whose families were taken from the village a week before the beginning of the war, which elicited sobbing of individual women.

Martial law won't last long, said the officer. The people will celebrate Christmas under the volleys of victorious salutes.

After the speech, Kuryk's first cousin Dmytro Uhryn brought the officer bread and salt on an embroidered cloth with a small flag pinned to it, woven with blue and yellow wool thread. The German somewhat fastidiously pinched the kalach bread and pushed it away together with Uhryn in the direction of a junior officer, directing him to stand behind him.

After the open meeting the Germans organized entertainment accompanied by mouth organs on the village pastureland. But the people for some reason weren't amused, they just silently and non-judgmentally watched the really young soldiers, who tried hard to spin several village girls and young women during the dance, and quietly whispered to each other.

The Germans camped in the village for a short time and didn't do great harm to the people, in the same way the people of Cheremoshne didn't do harm to them either, except for the poor girl Annytsia, who for years had been weak in the head, and walked through the village with rags ablaze on the tip of a pole so that the pole seemed to be a giant torch by evening in the dark village. The Germans locked up Annytsia for this for the night in the cellar of the commandant's headquarters, and in the morning, figuring out that she wasn't of completely sound mind, released her on the recognizance of her relatives.

Before their departure they again gathered the people near the church, and the same senior officer announced that their unit was forced to move further, and there, in Cheremoshne the German said it like that, in Cheremoshne they'll be leaving their allies—representatives of the Romanian wartime administration, whom the local people know well, and the German expects that they will be met well. The mention of the Romanian administration dragged out of the people the next recollection—about the beech switches—"forty whacks" for insubordination and reluctance to *vorbesti romanesti*[49]—and some faces in the crowd turned a little sour.

This time the German didn't organize merrymaking on the pastureland—he just marched in the direction of Vyzhnytsia behind covered green tractor trucks, and the people of Cheremoshne took to their work as before. Because no one abolished looking after the farm animals, hay cutting, tree felling, the birth of children, and the burial of the deceased for working people. Even during wartime.

The same as before the war, and maybe, even worse, the coarse, pigskin bast shoes of the new-old Romanian administration particularly were discordant with the waxed boots of the Germans, who had disappeared. But in Cheremoshne they saw even worse: more than one well-off *gazda* often took a poor guy as an ally, in order to have more influence in the village, or more likely, pure physical strength. The same or even more burning beech switches were the new-old way along with general and categorical prohibitions of any kind of politicking now.

The Germans still constantly remained in Cheremoshne on the other side of the river—and some Cheremoshnians from this side, while visiting their family or

---

49 Meaning: "to speak Romanian."

lying that they're visiting, remained there and voluntarily begged to go to work in Germany together with the Galician youth, whom they first took to the rail line, and beyond that—God only knows where... The Romanians from that side didn't encourage these kinds of activities from their allies—and thereafter under the pretext of martial law, they sharply restricted the possibility of contact with people located mirror-like on the other side of the Cheremosh.

...In short time the Romanians took away the men of a suitable age from the village to *concentrare* camps. In other words, they mobilized the subjects of the Romanian government for war. More precisely, for their army.

The hand mill of war kept grinding....

...Mykhailo right then was drying boards for woodworking when in his yard there stood....

Who would you have thought came to inform Mykhailo about mobilization to the army? Correct. The pre-war chief of the gendarmerie and border post, Lieutenant Lupul, who now was the senior representative of the military authorities in Cheremoshne.

"Lord help us, *domnul* Mihai!" He gave a greeting, closing the gate from inside on the hasp.

"Thank you for your good word!" Mykhailo answered bent over a piece of wood, sensing something sharply tearing off inside him.

The men for some time silently and without blinking simply stared into each other's eyes, and after that silently shook each other's hand, and then Lupul took off his military cap, sat down in the middle of the yard on the boards arranged in rows, gesturing to Mykhailo to sit down.

"You've come to take me to the war?" Emotionlessly, as though this didn't concern him, Mykhailo asked in Romanian, sitting down next to him.

Lupul didn't answer. Mykhailo was silent as well.

"Before going off to the war, you should invite me to your house for food and drink…," somewhat unusually the military man began to laugh, in a good way.

While Matronka was setting the table, the child, chatty like a magpie, sat down on the lieutenant's lap facing him, tugging at the woven plaits on his uniform and gazing into his eyes. Ordinarily, Mykhailo would have smacked the child on her fingers, but this time he kept sitting, heavily placing his large palms on the edge of the table, for some reason he kept looking at the door and from time to time sighed.

"*Doamno* Matrona!" Lupul said when the table was covered with soup plates, and lowered the chatty child from his lap. "Excuse me, but I'd like to speak with Mihai in private."

Tears started to flow one after another like rain along Matronka's face. Mykhailo shuddered. Matronka hadn't cried in a long time.

"Don't cry, *domno*…," the lieutenant tried to calm her as gently as possible, but she was already in the entryway.

"When should I get my rucksack ready for the road?" Mykhailo looked at Lupul with eyes that, it seemed, would also suddenly pour out tears.

"I haven't come to take you to the war, Mihai."

Mykhailo began to choke up from what he unexpectedly just heard.

"Who's going to take me?"

"While I'm here, no one will take you. When I'm not here, then anything can happen."

"What have I done to you that you're joking with me like this?" Mykhailo crumpled the edge of the tablecloth, but you could sense him seething.

"I'm not joking," Lupul said, without touching his food at all. "Mihai, I'm a person who doesn't joke. I'm a solider. I said I'm not going to take you—that means what I said."

"And why aren't you going to take me? You're taking away people my same age."

Lupul thought for a bit, and then looked right into Mykhailo's eyes:

"You see, Mihai, I doubt the war will end even without you there. And someone needs to keep order among the civilians. You think that only military people keep order among the people?... So here I'm really counting on you. Just children, old people, and cripples are left in the village, and if something would happen while the cannons are pounding at the front, there would be no one to come to the rescue.

"But can you do this?" Mykhailo was surprised.

"I can't. But you won't be writing on the picket fence about our conversation. All the more so, you've already been punished: you have a wife who's not healthy. A young child. You have a reasonable excuse."

"She's better now...," he tried to object unconvincingly.

Lupul interrupted him:

"And then... you're not entirely reliable for military service."

153

Out of surprise Mykhailo began to choke a second time. "Why is that?!"

"Have you forgotten under what circumstances and how your wife disappeared?" The Romanian asked somehow so readily, it seemed to Mykhailo, almost carelessly, as though he had disappeared together with Matronka; it was as if it were not a mystery for Mykhailo.

"What does my wife have to do with that?"

"What, don't you know?!" The lieutenant was truly astonished, now disconcerted by something.

"About what?"

Lupul sighed in the same way he did back then, when Mykhailo had come to announce that Matronka had disappeared:

"Strictly speaking, your wife has nothing to do with it. Yes, I just remembered she was missing, but who knows, maybe she's some kind of agent... And I truthfully don't have the right not to take you to the army, Mihai. But let this be only the greatest of my sins before his Excellency our king, great Romania, and the Lord God. My brother perished on the front, and he left behind little children. If you can keep from orphaning other people's children, then you have to do that."

Tomorrow come over to my post. We're going to replace the floor and door. Fungus has eaten through the floor completely...."

*

...On that day Mykhailo's hand, as heavy as a stone, for the first time counted Matronka's ribs.

154

In the wee hours of the morning, Mykhailo took the child to her godmother Maria, shut the gate and house with locks, shuttered the windows, tied Matronka's braid around a small bench in the room farthest from the road, put her on her knees and took an Austrian strap in his hands.

Merciful God... There's nothing worse than for a good man to have his mind clouded by suspecting his wife of betrayal. Neither blood that suddenly fills a person's mind during illness or disease, or physical pain, or the loss of someone close, or the greatest loss, or fire, or water do not act on a jealous man the way that one little thought, tiny as a flea, and sharp as a dagger: that another man—a stranger—knows his wife in a biblical way.

Until today Mykhailo would have spit in the face of anyone who would dare to say a bad word about his Matronka, who even after many years of marriage remained the very same gentle, Godfearing, nearly genuflecting before Mykhailo, the way she did in her maidenhood. She's unable to be without him for a day—maybe because she's weak. And he takes pity on her because the poor girl is weak. But you can't question her love for Mykhailo.

Once it seemed to Mykhailo that he would have stood on the fence and sung from a single thought: how every Saturday evening in the middle of the house she would fill up a great big wooden washtub with water, hot and fragrant from herbs, and then quickly hide herself in it, bashfully covering herself with her unplaited hair. In fact, there was no need for Matronka to cover herself: her thick hair fell heavily nearly all the way down to her heels, along her small, well-proportioned body, covering all its tiny hollows and tiny hills—to the point that Mykhailo's head became dizzy from passion. That mind-melting passion didn't pass for him even after Matronka's disappearance when for weeks without moving she lay and gazed at the ceiling. He even then would have walked on his knees to God Himself, if only God would stop the pain and give him back his wife, even if not entirely healthy, but his... his....

But today Mykhailo was stabbed without a knife and shot without a carbine: Lupul knows something about his wife that he, her married husband, doesn't know.

Well, surely, yes... In addition to that, why did Lupul speak so strangely and also chuckle?

Matronka was missing for three days? She was missing.

Who was the first who apparently went to look for her? Lupul's soldiers.

Mykhailo didn't think earlier why then at daybreak Lupul knocked at their window and seemingly also gave him some kind of advice? Maybe it was on purpose, because, maybe a Romanian was rolling around with her in the police station loft, or in some nearby forest hut, and then showed his gratitude—and said to dump his wife at a place where she could be easily found? So they dumped her in a place near the dam where a lot of people go. And now, you see, the Romanian has returned to the village, and isn't even sending Mykhailo to the war. So that people won't say that he sent a man to his death, and is chasing after his young wife. Maybe he wants to visit her in broad daylight, while Mykhailo is replacing the floor or the windows in the police station? Because why would he be so concerned about someone else's wife if he were not close to her?!

…He beat her the way you beat obstinate livestock: silently, without cursing or damning her, but in each blow placing all the strength of his hate and anger. Red sparks mercilessly jumped before his eyes—and he thought that bad blood was already filling his brain, and he wanted as quickly as possible to free himself from its heat, so as not to die here in front of Matronka. And Mykhailo beat his wife more vigorously—until his hand began to hurt, and he put the strap in his other hand.

…Matronka didn't beg. Didn't scream. It meant she was guilty, because she didn't even ask why he was beating her. She just bit her hair with her mouth and quietly moaned after each blow, until her exhausted head fell unconscious on the bench.

Mykhailo brought his wife back to consciousness with water and picked up the strap again….

It was already late when he poured a bucket of water on himself right by the well that he felt a wild surge of physical pain, as though someone suddenly had led *him* away bloody from the bench and had untied *his* wet and sweaty hair.

Even if he had wanted to, he couldn't explain to the Lord God Himself what had happened to him, and for what reason he, in fact, had so cruelly treated his wife. Mykhailo remembered that the lieutenant asked him something again about the disappearance of his wife long ago. And he asked something else innocent.

…Poor Mykhailo stood for the entire night on his knees before Matronka's bed and, wringing his hands, kept asking her:

"Tell me the truth, Matronka, what happened to you then?"

Turned to the wall, she weakly uttered:

"I already told you: I don't remember anything. I remember I fell. Other than that—I remember nothin'."

...From that time on jealously began to gnaw at Mykhailo. For someone who has never been jealous, it's hard to explain in simple words how a man can go crazy in a split second from what he always imagines he sees or hears.

...Sometimes it seemed to Mykhailo that it would be easier for him to chop off his finger than to walk everywhere behind his wife spying. Just think about it, even to the water closet. But he couldn't do anything, not so much with himself, but rather with that awful muddiness that each time filled his head when he looked at Matronka covered with her unbraided hair in the washtub, imagining someone else's hand pushing aside the heavy hair from her breasts.

Once long ago, when he was still working as a hired laborer, lightning hit Mykhailo in the pasture—and he almost ended up speaking with the angels. And now it seemed to him that it was easier to sense instant death than to carry in your heart that sudden torment that took away both sleep and peacefulness, and desire for life itself.

Jealousy, heavy, like the hand of a corpse, jealousy haunted Mykhailo—and he began to haunt his wife.

Matronka goes to Maria—Mykhailo, behind Maria's stable, will just gaze out from behind the wall, like a thief, and again hides like a thief. And until his wife goes home. Matronka goes to the tavern for salt—Mykhailo is already fixing the pole fence with his ax near it.

Even the four-year-old child who walked with Matronka, not letting go of the apron skirt for even a minute, could not save him from his loathsome conjectures and an even greater imagination. If need be, you could lull the child to sleep, Mykhailo thought, and found a way to follow his wife, leaving all the pressing work in the pen, to the point that people started to be surprised by him. Well, a man shouldn't follow a woman like this everywhere even if she's his wife and even if she's a little weak.

Only Matronka understood Mykhailo's torment—but she didn't show a sign: she tried to keep to the yard, and all the more kept silent. They rake this way behind the house—and in such a way as though two deaf people had been hired to work at the same time, only the child chirps, like a magpie, and gathers weeds behind them. They nearly simultaneously will kiss the child on her head or on her brow, silently smiling to themselves—and they continue to rake and remain silent.

Sometimes it seemed to Mykhailo that he was letting go of his jealousy, just as Matronka got over her weakness bit by bit. Then he almost joyfully crossed himself wherever he was, even if he were in the middle of the road and, joyful, almost ran to the house as though he were tipsy.

But it was worth it to see how slowly, as though with broken legs, Matronka and the child walked to the meadow for the livestock, and the black fog of suspicion spread all over his body wracked by mistrust; and he already didn't know whether to go spying, or to sit here like a post in the middle of the pen until Lupul or someone else comes again and tells him to go take his wife.

Mykhailo stopped far away past the meadow bushes and looked till his eyes hurt at Matronka gazing at the other side of the river. Little, just as tiny as she was before the wedding, she lowered her feet down and, spreading out her hands apart, held onto a stone with her palms, as though she were afraid that someone will suddenly drag her down. Then she raised her palm up to shield her brow and began to stare intently at the other shore.

Oh, this was most dangerous—for Matronka's ritual of silent contemplation of the village on the other side was incomprehensible to Mykhailo. Mykhailo approached closer to the dam, put his own palm up to shield his eyes—and again blind wrath drove into his heart to the point he began to feel faint, as though from the premonition of mortal danger. He gazed at the other shore to the point that it hurt his eyes—but, besides rustling bushes and individual figures in the gardens and courtyards of the mirror-like reflecting Cheremoshne, he didn't find anything there.

What does she see there that Mykhailo doesn't, and what it is that doesn't even catch his eye?

Why is it that her always smooth brow at that moment is creased with wrinkles, like the hundred-year-old Maria Trandachykha?

What draws her to this dam?

After a certain amount of time Matronka slowly got up, took the child in her arms, and at full speed ran to the house, urging a cow from behind with a switch.

And Mykhailo walked through the meadow till late. He didn't know himself why he did that. It seemed to him that at any moment he would see some kind of sign left by Matronka, then sometimes the thought pierced him that somewhere in the greenery there must be a flattened bed of grass with the outlines of a human body.

And once there during the day Mykhailo met Lieutenant Lupul in the meadow. He was sitting approximately in the same spot where Matronka loved to sit down, and for some reason he was guiding a slender switch along his bare toes, as though he were tickling or caressing himself.

*

...Who knows how Mykhailo's sudden and, we'll say in advance, groundless jealousy would have ended if not... if not for the war suddenly changing life and... not for history, which never stops riding over people with its wheels....

But this time Lupul abandoned the village with his soldiers in the middle of the night without saying farewell, and without even closing their former police station.

Accompanied by the far-off thunder of the cannonade, which even the somewhat deaf Tanasiy Maksymiuk could hear at night in Cheremoshne, now the German police returned already with policemen. And some of the local *gazdas* during this in-between time and yet another temporary anarchy not only managed to profit from the possessions left by the Romanian administration, but even smashed the windows in Yuz Rozenfeld's former estate to pieces, where under the second Romanian

occupation Florya, the grandson of the former Cheremoshne landowner Floreskul, was the master here and
disappeared together with Lupul's soldiers, leaving in the
lurch a great amount of his belongings.

...The next week immediately after, when complete
disorder reigned in the village, since the Romanians had
gone and no one else had yet come, Matronka, as always,
was in church at mass. For years she invariably stood
in the first row of the women's seating section, closer to
the icon of St. Nicholas the Wonderworker,[50] and strove
not to raise her eyes at anyone other than at Mykhailo,
who stood similarly in the first row among the house-
holders, and at the priest. But this time for some reason
during the church service her eyes lingered on a female
figure, who had draped a cloth on the icon of the Mother
of God in the middle of the church. Matronka couldn't
say at first why she for so long examined the woman,
who so fervently had kissed the icon as though it were
a living person, as though she were striving for as long
as possible to keep in view of the entire church. But after a minute she realized that she didn't see the woman,
but just the sleeves of her blouse, evidently not just for
Sunday but rather more festive, maybe even for Easter,
with thick red-yellow-green roses embroidered with fine
cross-stitches, and with large round tassel ties. This tri-
ple-rose embroidery, unusual in Cheremoshne, reminded Matronka of something really dire, and perhaps even
tragic; and now in the middle of the service, before the
eyes of the Holy Father, with hands folded to pray the

---

50   Literally "St. Nicholas the Peacemaker" (Uhodnyk), who is better
known in the West as St. Nicholas the Wonderworker or St. Nikolaos of
Myra.

"Our Father," Matronka couldn't remember what in fact so struck her, that her heart even began to beat more rapidly. She had already seen a similar blouse on someone somewhere before. But no, not similar, but exactly this one, here on her left sleeve the top petal was two times wider than the lower one. Maybe, the embroiderer didn't take the trouble to redo it from the start, in order to make it even, and on the right—the petals are identical. But then that blouse was not on Vasyuta Kalynych, but on someone else... well, yes! Yilena, the eldest daughter of Kuryk, had worn that blouse during Easter before the war. And Dzodz's wife used to wear this apron skirt at Christmas, and today it's hanging on Mrs. Kalynych like on a picket fence.

Merciful Lord... the childless Mrs. Kalynych had so much of her own clothing, there would be enough for three marriageable maidens. Then why does she need other people's blouses and apron skirts? And how did they end up on her, when their mistresses were taken from the village already several years ago?!

Matronka had never left the church alone before the end of the service, but now she quietly slid out among the people, knowing that Mykhailo would catch up to her right away.

"...Mykhailo, sweetie, did you see, she crossed herself and said the 'Our Father,' she covered the Mother of God, and neither her face nor conscience were burning, and her fingers weren't folded! How can such a thing be, Mykhailo sweetie? What has happened with these people that they are so unkind not even to strangers but to their own people?! How do these people think to go on living and not fear that their sins will be passed on to their children?! It's not only me who has eyes and a memory! And are other people blind? And why did they all keep silent, and no one left the church? Why?! Everyone saw!" Matronka cried as if she had been beaten right before.

Mykhailo sat near her by the wall of the house on a bench and wiped away her tears with his hand.

"You were a witness, Mykhailo sweetie: no matter how angry Mrs. Danyliuk was, back then she didn't go to steal Kuryk's belongings. But this one went, though she had full storerooms of everything, and the Kuryks had never pestered her about anything, but she went. And now she makes the sign of the cross to God.

"Matronka, I'm begging you, don't cry. Your head will begin to ache," Mykhailo appealed, reproaching himself for his stupid jealously, which again made Matronka tearful and sensitive to any injustice, one not even her own.

"Mykhailo sweetie, but it belongs to someone else! It's covered in tears. And people aren't afraid of sinning. Then why would you pray then? Will those words reach God, and will they be heard by God? My skin would burn up under a stolen blouse... But tell me, Mykhailo dear, how does God look at this and why doesn't He punish bad people in a way that everyone could see?!..."

"Such are the times, woman...," Mykhailo just sighed.

*

...And the next day a German unit entered the village and without any particular formalities ordered the people to prepare immediately for evacuation from the front that was approaching closer to Cheremoshne. The first line of defense was supposed to pass through the village.

The Germans set aside several trucks for people with household tableware, and they told them to leave their farm animals out to graze.

The strong village *gazdas* listened to the German, further taking council with each other, and decided to drive as much livestock through the forest as possible. They determined who would drive cattle and who would reconnoiter, and then they hit the road. You wouldn't say this was easy or safe, but to evacuate to an unknown place for no one knows how long, without milk, meat, and also with children... this isn't the *gazda* way. You need more than just crab apples to feed children. But as soon as the front enters the village, good luck trying to find your cows and sheep....

And by the time the *gazdas* drove their cattle and pigs into faraway Konyatyn and its surrounding farmsteads, they already needed to return. The front unprecedentedly in quick tempo passed around Cheremoshne and didn't touch it, and moved to the West along other lands.

And the Cheremoshne drivers and shepherds turned the cattle back, for the umpteenth time, cursing the war, the Germans, and their fate.

When, tired by the long road, people returned to their farmsteads, in the village other Soviets were bringing order, announced Tanasiy Maksymiuk, who didn't evacuate to Konyatyn, but had hidden in the village in his smokehouse.

In place of all the seventeen Jewish taverns, burnt ruins turned terribly black, and on them now, not fearful of people, black ravens were walking, looking for some carrion for food and raking up the hot ashes almost to the sky.

Several houses were totally ransacked, so that their previous owners were forced to beg among the people.

The widow Mrs. Yurchak gave birth in a cellar without anyone's help to a little boy fathered by a Romanian policeman, right before the departure of the last car with the German squadron.

And the bred cow left in the garden by Mrs. Bundyak gave birth to a little baby bull, but for some reason went mad out of her bovine mind—and now she was constantly foaming at the mouth, and the baby bull already was waving his black and white tail.

...Life and war continued simultaneously, at the same time dependent on and independent from one another.

*

...On Sunday when people were coming out of church, the military surrounded them with weapons in a semi-circle. Armed soldiers stood from the church bell tower all the way to the porch of the village council building on the other side of the road, creating a living human corridor.

The people started to stamp their feet, huddling together, like sheep herded into a pen. Some returned to the church, others entered the bell tower, creating unbelievable stuffiness and crowding there, and one of the more resourceful men—clambered up between the bells and with all his strength sounded the alarm.

You could ring all day long and it wouldn't change anything—outside the doorway of the bell tower there were two military guys, and between them a woman.

They were taking people to the village council building and didn't release a single one of them.

With her right hand Matronka clenched her child's little hand, and with the left took Mykhailo's. They walked that way through the formation of the soldiers with machine guns—the three of them holding each other's hands.

In the middle of the room of the former village groundskeeper stood two large desks. A military man sat at each one. From behind, two more military men loomed with side-holstered pistols.

A senior officer paced about the room, shifting his revolver from hand to hand. An authorized agent from the regional MGB (The Ministry for State Security), Major Didushenko, had a bad reputation in Cheremoshne. From time to time he would lead a raid into the village like a fury, and several people would disappear with him regardless of gender, property status, or age. Some returned with bruised or broken fingers or burnt skin, many haven't returned to this day. And whoever would return kept his mouth shut. After Didushenko people walked around like thrashed sheep: that is to say, they had a living soul, but on the other hand it didn't do them any good.

"Come forward, come forward," Didushenko nearly bowed down to Matronka, Mykhailo, and the child, pointing his hand in the direction of the desks. "Sign in, wherever you want. Matronka took a look at Mykhailo, Mykhailo—at Matronka, and then—at the desks. On one a stack of white paper rose, on another a single sheet of paper with writing on. It shone white.

"Over there," Didushenko pointed with his revolver at the desk with the single sheet, "one of your *gazdas* has signed up for deportation, for resettlement, one word. He says the climate here is too warm for him, so he desires to cool off his head a little bit, and at the same time to show his family with many children the wide world. And over there," he pointed the revolver at the piles of papers covered with writing, "people of their own free will have shown the desire to go to the collective farm and turn in their cattle, their farm implements, and everything they don't need in their household, and begin to farm not individually, but as a group. So come up and choose where you want to go. It's a big choice," the officer began to laugh, winking at Matronka in a somehow vulgar way.

Matronka shielded her child with her body, standing in front of her, and Mykhailo kept shifting his weight from one foot to the other, crumpling his hat in his hands.

"You see, we can finally say that a peaceful life has been established in this region. The last bandits and their accomplices have given themselves up to Soviet power. Some have turned themselves in with the help of the people. And those who took too long to think about it— sorry, that's life. Soviet power loves order and calm at its rear guard. The local people support us. And whoever hesitates—we'll help them begin to see clearly.

"So what are you, Mykhailo, your name's Mykhailo, right?" Didushenko addressed him sharply: "You can rest assured: we've already designated you as the collective farm stock man. In the collective farm you'll be collecting dairy products and then transporting them to the butter factory in Vyzhnytsya. The people in the village have recommended you themselves. They say you can't find a more honest man in the district. For the time being the procurement office will be in your house, and then we'll build warehouses. So, be so kind," he pushed a clean sheet of paper closer to the edge of the desk and gave Mykhailo a pencil. "Write a statement expressing your desire to be accepted into the Kirov Collective Farm, I'll dictate it to you. And we'll look it over, we'll think it over, and maybe, accept you. There is a lot of competition. You see yourself," and again he pointed to the papers covered with writing.

"At the same time sign up your wife... Oh, what a pretty child!" He walked behind Matronka and stroked the child with his revolver along her head till she hid her face in her mother's apron skirt....

"What's your name, child?..."

*

...In the morning, on the second day after the Feast of St. Dimitry, an entire truckload of soldiers with weapons was brought into Cheremoshne.

And again the villagers were driven to the village council building. It was cold and really windy. Snow mixed with rain began to sprinkle—so the people dressed in winter clothes: in quilted coats and old coarse woolen coats. They separated the men, who were ordered to be there without fail, from the women—and now two black groups were hunched at the rear of the village council building.

Next to the black wall, right under a large window were sitting two corpses: a really young guy and an altogether young girl, you might say, almost a little girl. The wind was stirring the hair on their heads—and it seemed they were alive, and just were afraid of opening their eyes from shame. They were stark naked, the way their mother had given birth to them; they were propping up the village council building, and at the same time propping up each other's heads.

The boy on the right, and the girl on the left had bullets through their temples. And if you didn't know it was dried blood, you might have thought that they had tied a small dried rose by their hair.

From between the boy's legs stuck out a sawn-off gun, as though it were aiming at the sky.

Between the girl's legs that were spread so widely, where you could see a birthmark on the inside of her thigh, a pinecone stuck out, covering the ruddy strands of the hair of her shame. Instead of breasts, two deep holes blackened with dried blood. One of the girl's eyes had been knocked out and also gaped horribly from the plucked out hole.

Didushenko stood on the porch in a long leather coat. He smoked and silently sized up the people from head to toe.

The women were crying, hiding their faces in the sleeves of their quilted coats.

The men stood with their heads sunken down.

It was quiet—it even seemed you could hear the snow falling and streaming like tears onto the murdered youngsters.

The boy was from Cheremoshne. The son of Yurko Ohronnyk. His name was Ivan, and his nickname Falcon.

When the German troops were still in the village, Ivan's guerilla unit smashed up their provisions wagon. The insurgents took out the guards, placing each of them face to the ground, and put an egg on their backs, threatening them saying they were grenades. While the Germans lay there stock still, Ivan's boys did what they had come to do well. And if not for the evacuation, who knows how the Germans would have dealt with the local people.

And from that time on, Ivan was master in the forest, and at night in the surrounding villages of Bukovyna and Halychyna. The new authorities felt the sting of his work, each day losing a policeman, then the head of the collective farm. Other Soviets, as the mountain people now named the new-old authorities, promised big money to anyone who would reveal Ivan's location or his possible contacts.

In the village they knew that Ivan's guerilla unit was the last one left in their district: that was 1950. But neither systematic round-ups nor cunning ambushes led to a single one of Ivan's hideouts. Good people informed whom they needed to inform about the fact that the only person in the world who knew his son's abode—was his father. Thus Ohronnyk's house and Yurko himself were put under surveillance by very sharp-sighted local people as well as by countless military men. On the other hand, there were no results: it was unknown how Yurko disappeared from the village, but he always returned home during broad daylight with empty saddlebags on his back, as though he were striding along the road after tiresome and successful bargaining at a bazaar. He walked along the street, completely indifferent, as though he were emptied like his saddlebags, and he looked in front of himself without greeting anyone and not answering anyone's greetings. So one day the MGB guys dug up the Ohronnyks' entire yard and turned the house upside down, but couldn't find a secret passage. Then they took the old man to Vyzhnytsya to the MGB office. Ohronnyk had been imprisoned for several months already, and till this day the village knew that he didn't sell out his son. Surely someone else sold him out if Ivan, now dead, was propping up the village council building.

The young girl, evidently, was from out of town, because no one could recognize her. Some whispered that she was a messenger, and that, maybe, she had even shown them Ivan's bunker. Others nodded their heads, silently hinting at something else. But either way, nearly the entire village right now was gravely silent, inhaling deeply and holding its breath from fear.

In the meantime Didushenko stepped off the porch and barked something unintelligible to an armed soldier who was standing next to the corpses.

The latter, not thinking for long, ran up to the wall, and with both of his hands first dragged away the girl, placing her on her back nearly right in front of the people. And then on top of her, face down, he put the boy. Ivan's head from the back was completely crushed to pieces. The wind lifted up the remains of his soft blonde hair only on the crown of his head—and from this kind of horror, it seemed, the people's hair was also standing on end, because several men from time to time smoothed their bare heads with their palms.

"Well, what?" Didushenko asked, tossing his cigarette on the bodies. "Have you recognized who that whore is who's been bringing food to this *bandera*?"[51] He grabbed the first who was standing in the group of men by the chin. "Do you know her? You don't know! And I don't!" And I don't care now who this slut is. Love to the grave!" He started to laugh through his teeth and spat. "They'll soon be bringing one more. He wanted to be smarter than everyone. It won't work!" Didushenko screamed, walking back and forth in front of the frightened people. "It'll be like this with everyone who dares to oppose or thwart Soviet power."

...In the meantime a cart rode up to the yard. From it soldiers pulled off the dead Yurko Ohronnyk and positioned him in the same way by the wall of the village council building, on the spot where the corpses had just been removed. The dead father with his broken neck looked at the horror of this inhuman torture of his murdered son—and the mute and petrified people looked at the three corpses with eyes that knew for certain that they would be tortured to death after these unfortunate ones.

Old Ohronnyk was bare to his waist, with his arms chopped off at his elbows. Yurko's face also was a bloody mess, and if on his head, among his shorn hair, there had not been a bump from the day he was born, maybe people wouldn't have recognized the old man.

"I'll tell you myself how this damned pig wanted to wind us around his finger!" Didushenko spattered the people with spit. "Because all the same you'll twist my

---

51   From the last name of Stepan Bandera (1909-1959), who was reviled by the Soviets as the leader of the Organization of Ukrainian Nationalists and the Ukrainian Insurgent Army, which conducted guerilla warfare against them. Bandera was murdered in exile by an agent of the Soviet secret police in Munich in 1959.

words. And I'll tell the truth, so that you can fix it in your mind: it will be this way with everyone who aids these bandits. This old fart for three months resisted showing us his son's bunker. But we are patient. No one is as patient as the Soviet authorities and their representatives!" Didushenko screamed without catching his breath. "And then he tried to fool us and led us to Chortove Urvyshche.[52] This Austrian fucker tried to jump into the precipice together with our officer, to whom he was shackled with handcuffs. It failed! We helped him fly down by himself. And we helped him leave his hands with us. For that we have sharp bayonets.

We pulled out our comrade by his overcoat, together with the old man's hands. But we also pulled out this bastard from the bottom to show one more time what kind of fate awaits everyone who tries to deceive us even in the smallest way! Everyone!

The Soviet authorities hear everything, see everything, and know everything, because they have ears and eyes everywhere. And they will get anybody out of any bunker. Like the way they got these two bastards and their slut. They wanted love to the grave—and now they have it. And they have witnesses….

Look here and tell everyone who has ears, but hasn't yet understood: the last band and its head have been liquidated today on this territory! The la-a-st!"

---

52   Meaning "the Devil's Ravine."

*

...In the middle of the night they knocked three times. No, they scratched three times the way the branch of a tree near a house, swayed by the wind, scratches a window pane.

Half-asleep, Mykhailo thought that mice were making holes in the floor. But the knocking-scratching repeated after an equal interval of time—and Mykhailo's heart began to beat more intensely. Nothing good has ever come from nighttime knocking. He covered the sleepy Matronka up to her neck with a blanket, and, throwing on his clothes that were within reach, he went to the entryway. The entryway was cluttered with benches, cans, and barrels, so that Mykhailo gropingly, in order not to rattle or knock into anything with his heavy legs, reached the door. Forged with iron, the heavy oak door from the entryway to the porch was locked from the inside with two iron latches and one key made of yew that was stronger than any iron key.

"Who's there?" Mykhailo pressed his lips to the door, at the same time pressing his ear to the door and turning one latch.

"Let me in, *gadza* Mykhailo, it's one of your people...," a quiet man's voice could be heard from outside.

The two men who entered the house in boots, quilted coats, and Mazepa[53] caps with sawn-off rifles were not familiar to either Mykhailo or Matronka. Several more remained outside.

---

53   Military caps in the style of what Cossack Hetman Ivan Mazepa wore in the early 18th century. For photographs of the caps worn by members of the Ukrainian Insurgent Army in the 20th century see: http://forum.milua. org/viewtopic.php?p=60506.

Matronka, wrapping herself in a large wool scarf, tried to turn the lamp up higher.

"Don't, ma'am," the tallest one stopped her. "The less light, the better. We didn't come here to look at the light."

The child began to stir on the sleeping ledge over the oven. The man made his voice quieter:

"We're not going to say a lot. We've come for some cheese, *brynza* sheep milk cheese, and butter. And whatever else you can share. You, *gazda*, have an entire storehouse of those Russky goods, and we don't have any more reserves."

Mykhailo sighed at the top of his voice:

"That's the people's goods."

"True—it's the people's, but it's going to the Russkies. We're not going to take everything."

Now Matronka sighed at the top of her voice:

"And what will he say tomorrow at the collective farm?" She pointed her hand at Mykhailo.

"He'll say they broke in during the middle of the night from the forest, they carried out a pogrom in the house, they frightened us with weapons, robbed and disappeared, like *shcheznyk* demons.[54] On top of that, they punched him a few more times. You'll inform them yourself at daybreak. And they'll do nothing to you. They won't grow any poorer from it. And from us and from all true Ukrainians you'll have gratitude.

It became really quiet in the house. Just the child on the oven sleeping ledge turned to her other side.

"And on Saturday you'll butcher a pig. We'll come for the fresh pork. You can't be angry with us—we haven't

54 Demonic, mischievous creatures from Carpathian folklore, who are invisible and appear and disappear.

taken anything from you yet. And people help us any way they can. Otherwise they would have long ago killed us."

"Last fall Didushenko said that…," the tallest man didn't let him finish:

"…What he said was stupid. You see yourself—we exist. There aren't many of us any longer, but still quite a few. And we won't give them any peace for as long as we can. We're from Holub's squadron. Maybe you've heard of us? We're more active in Galicia. And the people of Bukovyna are helping us with food and clothes. They're helping us a lot. Now it's your turn, *gazda*."

Matronka wringed her hands so much that you could hear her fingers crack, and she started to sob at the top of her voice unable to contain herself.

Mykhailo, thinking it over, just said:

"We have no other choice…."

…It was just before the break of day as the military guys filled the yard. They rummaged through every corner of the farmstead plots, they banged buckets in the stable, tore off wood planks in the barn, and from time to time briefly called to one another.

From two of the house's windows broken shards of glass stuck out.

Mykhailo and Matronka sat by the wall on a low bench, not looking at each other and not even saying anything to each other. Mykhailo took a drag of the damp tobacco. Matronka sat motionless, with her hands clasped together at her chest.

The child was playing by the woodshed, setting out wooden soup bowls with spoons near her pots full of holes.

In the yard, despite the presence of such a number of people, a flame-red rooster was grinding a gray hen, and a white tailless kitty cat tumbled in the dust, as though he were scratching his back.

They waited for Didushenko to come from Vyzhnytsya.

And while they were waiting, they didn't really question anyone except for two military guys in shoulder belts across their shoulders who walked right over to the immediate neighbors.

Didushenko wasn't alone when he arrived: there was one other military guy with him—a short one, on the heavyset side, with darting eyes, like those of a skunk, and deep bald spots. On him somehow awkwardly, as though there was room to grow into it, hung a dark-green uniform with shoulder belts; his riding breeches stuck out as though they were windblown, and his Russian leather boots glistened.

Whether it was from lengthy nervous anticipation, or maybe, from being faint from hunger, but, just as the MGB guys step into the pen and hailed, Matronka's surrounding world went topsy-turvy, and she fell down unconscious right onto the threshold.

While the soldiers were pouring water on her, having given her before that a few slaps in the face for her to come to, and while they were calming down the child frightened by such a spectacle, Didushenko interrogated Mykhailo himself.

The major sat at the table, leafing through some kind of papers, and then for a long time fixed his eyes on Mykhailo. He stood in the middle of the house, drawing his head into his shoulders, and held his arms next to his body nearly at attention. However, he didn't remove his gaze.

"We-e-ll...," Didushenko slowly uttered, as though he were releasing a few smoke rings from his cigarette. "So, you are saying, they carried out a pogrom, punched you a few times, and also robbed you...."

"I already told you...."

"How many of them do you say there were, two?" Didushenko asked again, tapping his fingers on the table.

"Two in the house and outside, it seems like two. I didn't see any more."

"...So's they came like this, you peacefully let them inside your door, and they, the cutthroats, started breaking the windows, and scaring the dogs...."

"No, they first took from the storehouses what they needed, and while they were leaving, the last one broke the windows. And I let them in the house, cause what was I supposed to do? I have a little child... and a wife... and they had sawn-off rifles."

"We-e-e-ll...," Didushenko spoke this time somehow suspiciously—slowly, peacefully, without cursing. "You say four of them took, how many, Mykhailo, how many chunks of cheese? Twenty chunks, two kilos each? Plus a tub of whipped butter. And how much butter was there?" Didushenko again looked at his papers. "Aha, half a hundredweight. I s-e-e... the sour cream is gone as well. How many buckets, Mykhailo? Five? And in the bucket... Aha! And also two barrels of *brynza* sheep milk cheese... You hear, Mykhailo," the major now drilled him with his eyes without blinking, but didn't get up from behind the table: "And what would happen, listen, if you didn't wag your tail and play the dummy, and said what really happened?! You, my man, don't know how to lie. And swindling isn't your thing. Because you are telling me and lying, and it doesn't come out right for me—and that's it…."

"I've told you…," for the first time he lowered his eyes down. "I told you how it was. I saw four of them. Maybe there were more of them on the side. But two of them took stuff and carried it outside. They're strangers, not from our village. And they didn't talk a lot. And what happened after that, where they went—from where they came, they didn't tell me, and I didn't look. Maybe they had a wagon.

"You sa-a-id… Listen, my man, then why didn't your neighbors hear the uproar in your house? Your child didn't cry out of fright, your wife didn't wail, you didn't call anyone for help. Here they rob the collective farm's procurement chief—and not a word fell from his lips, as though he had invited the guests himself. And the neighbors didn't hear any wagons. And the policeman didn't hear or see anything. And "little hawks"[55] were patrolling the village. No one found any trampled tracks. What are they—giant people, who step from hill to hill and don't leave any tracks? Even more, you say, that they were not from the village. And you didn't run to your neighbors right after that. You said that this happened after midnight, but one man saw that your windowpanes flew out before dawn, but no one came out of the house, so, it was

---

55   *Yastrubky* (meaning "little hawks) were youngsters who helped the Soviet secret police, the MGB, to battle against the Stepan Bandera supporters in Western Ukraine.

as if an unclean force had broken those windows. Maybe you, Mykhailo, forgot something out of fear, think about it a bit more... try to remember and tell the truth, and we'll wait."

"What is there to think about here? Maybe some drunken guy told you that and can't remember when it was. And I didn't have any reason to scare the neighbors. What, could they have helped return the cheese and butter? I went to inform you, and people will spread it around to everyone else without me."

Didushenko's comrade didn't barge in on the interrogation, but just sat there and listened, folding his hands as though he were about to say the "Our Father," tapped the tips of his fingers, and smacked his tongue. Then he stepped out of the house, and when after a bit of time returned, he was evidently satisfied by something.

"Let's go," he said to Didushenko, and all three men shuffled outside.

The drooping, completely weak-willed and even indifferent Matronka now was sitting on a log in the middle of the pen, covering her face down to her eyes with a scarf.

The child was standing near her, holding her hand on her mother's head.

Mykhailo stood near them.

The officer in riding breeches sat on a log three steps away and, smiling, silently pulled out something out of the pocket of his army shirt without lowering his eyes from the masters of the house. It was a green rooster lollipop on a long stick, with a luxurious crest and tail, lengthened and twisted up high.

The officer raised the rooster to his lips and one time slowly licked it all over its surface, so slowly, that a thick white coating became visible on his tongue. Then he licked the rooster a second time—for a long time leading the tip of his tongue first along the tail, then along the crest. He silently savored the lollipop with such pleasure that even the surprised Didushenko audibly gulped his saliva. Having sated himself, the officer pulled out of the pocket of his riding breeches one more—this time a red—rooster with the same twisted up tail and luxurious comb, and put it on his knee. Once again raising the green rooster to his lips and briefly licking it, he now exclusively kept looking at the child. Sucking on the green rooster in a way that you could hear the loud smacking of his tongue, the officer beckoned with his left index finger for the child to come to him.

And here Matronka shuddered, as though awakened from sleep, as though she were intent on not letting go of her child, but the child already was standing in front of the officer without taking her eyes away from the rooster on his knee.

"What's your name, little girl?" The man asked with a lively voice, coaxing to the point of unseemliness, looking at the child right in her eyes.

"Darusya, the daughter of Mykhailo Ilashchuk, the son of Petro."

"And how old are you, Darusya, daughter of Mykhailo Ilashchuk, the son of Petro, and how is it you are so smart?"

"The month after the Feast of the Presentation of Our Lord in the Temple I turned ten."

"And do you know the 'Our Father'?"

"Yes I do. And I also know the Creed."

"And do you like sweet candies?"

"I do."

The officer and child stared at one another, as though they were competing to see who would blink first.

The green rooster became smaller in the officer's mouth, losing one tail feather to the officer's quick tongue.

The little girl shifted her weight from one leg to the other and swallowed her saliva.

The officer lifted up the red rooster from his knees close to the child's lips, but didn't put it in her mouth.

"Darusya, your father said that some guys came to your place at night…."

The child kept looking at the green rooster that once again slowly hid in the man's mouth, first just what was left of the comb, and then completely disappeared. She blinked her eyes as though she were thinking about something.

"They came," she answered, following the red rooster sticking its luxurious comb into her tiny mouth.

Before she was even able to lick it properly, the red comb already jumped out of her mouth and began to jump in front of her nose.

With one hand the officer held the two roosters—the green one, nearly completely shrunken, and the red one as though bristling for battle—and with his other touched and stroked the child's two thick and long braids—all the way to her knees—tied with colored woolen bands.

"Darusya, who does your braids so beautifully?"

"My mom Matronka."

"You don't know how to braid them yourself?"

"I know how. Can I show you?"

The officer himself untied one of the bands on one of the braids, quickly unbraided it to the middle and transferred a silken bunch of hair into the child's hands:

"Show me."

The little girl quickly did one braid, tied it, fixed the second one, and then looked at the officer.

The red rooster again jumped onto the child's little tongue. And when the officer dragged it out one more time, the rooster was already tailless.

The officer began to laugh, twirling the lollipop in front of the child's eyes.

The little girl began to laugh too.

"Darusya, your mother—whose daughter is she?"

"Mama Matronka is the daughter of Ivan Yakiviuk, the son of Timofiy from Malyneshne."

"And those guys who came at night, did they beat up your father a lot?" The little girl shifted her eyes from the rooster to her father.

Her father stood behind her mother and stared at his feet.

Emotionless—as though she were dead—her mother sat there, without removing the scarf from her eyes. It was nearly completely wet.

"They didn't beat father."

"They didn't beat your father, but they did break the windows, right?"

"No, daddy broke the windows himself when the guys left."

"But your mommy cried? Right? And said to give the guys the *brynza* sheep milk cheese?"

"Mommy cried a lot. The guys said to give the *brynza*, but mommy didn't want daddy to give it to them."

Now the tailless red rooster at first jumped right into Darusya's little palm, and then ended up in her mouth. When it darted out of there already without a comb, the officer again asked:

"Darusya, and what else did the guys say to daddy?"

"They said to butcher a pig by Saturday."

The officer got up from the log, looking first at Didushenko, then at the child:

"That's good. There's time till Saturday... And now run off, sweet Darusya—daughter of Mykhailo Ilash-chuk, the son of Petro, to auntie Maria and play with little Slava. And give him a rooster too. For sure, he hasn't seen a rooster like this." And the officer pulled out of his riding breeches one more—this time a yellow—lollipop.

"...And where were you, Mykhailo, the son of Petro, getting ready to go?" Didushenko listlessly inquired, crushing his cigarette with his boot, when Mykhailo came out of the house with a backpack over his shoulder packed as though for the road.

Mykhailo looked without understanding what Didushenko was asking about.

"If to prison—then we don't need you there so you're fed for free. There are enough other parasites and slackers there. We won't need a lot." The major looked at the officer in riding breeches who was washing up right from the well's bucket as though after a hard day's work, snorting like a colt: "If by Saturday you can return twice the quota of milk products to the procurement facility—you'll stay home.

We have nowhere to rush. There's a ton of time till Saturday. Siberia won't warm up by then. If you don't get it—you yourself know… I don't have to tell you, a half-baked dunce.

And don't beat the child. A child is always fair… You have to think with your head, and if you think with your legs, then let your head suffer. It's obvious a stupid preacher man baptized you, Mykhailo. And don't forget: not a single person has been able to fool the Soviet authorities, you motherfucker. Didushenko doesn't know a cunning one like that, because a cunning one like that hasn't been born yet.

…Matronka hastily loaded things for departure. And then in the same way hastily laid them out in place. Then she lay down face first on her pillow and, without uttering a word, lay like that till nightfall.

Mykhailo put things in order in silence: inserted glass into the windows, swept the entryway, sorted the barrels and cans, and then sat in the yard by the wall—and he didn't let go of the pipe from his mouth, also till nightfall.

"I would have been better off poisoning such an unclean force in my womb or giving birth to a mute…," Matronka said maliciously without getting up from her bed.

Mykhailo put his hand on her head:

"God forbid, woman, what are you saying, the child isn't at fault…."

"Then who is?"

"The people who informed. And they just took advantage of the child. Someone informed before me. They informed about everything that happened. Maybe even one of those who came in the middle of the night. You see what's happening. People here know how to do good for another person, and they know well how to serve two at the same time. What they know how to do—they know how to do. But the child doesn't understand what's going on. We haven't taught our child to lie. And who knew that she heard everything?"

"But do you, Mykhailo, understand what's going on?!" Matronka screamed and cried, banging her head against the wall. "Do you understand?! How will we get out of this now?"

"I don't know, woman… But somehow we'll get out of this… God will help us."

Suddenly Matronka darted onto her feet and for the first time he could remember, she stood before Mykhailo as though she were threatening to strike him:

"Where is that God of yours, when he turned away from us like from the worst sinners? Why doesn't he turn away from one who does evil to someone else, and lives happily himself? What did I do wrong to God that He sent my tormenter to my home today? I thought that my tormenter had rotted away long ago for all my ordeals, and today he made an enemy out of my child? So then where is God, has he gone blind, Mykhailo, when I so earnestly prayed to him my entire life, and he took away your mind as well, because you beat me like livestock, and I had to remain silent?! You beat me for nothing, you know that yourself, and the one who is guilty came today to finish me off. And God didn't stop him."

"Stand up, Matronka," Mykhailo leaned his wife's head to his chest, sensing that yet one more ordeal, and maybe not the least terrifying one, was right now awaiting him. He took a really deep breath, as though he intended to go under water. "What are you saying, woman? What tormenter are you talking about?"

And then Matronka told Mykhailo the truth that had sealed her lips for ten years. All that time until today.

*

...For a long time that June evening Matronka walked around the dam far below looking for the cow that had suddenly disappeared, but the animal wasn't there. For some reason the water was foaming more than usual, and on the other side something seemed to be not right— alarming maybe? Freezing and with fraught nerves, she already wanted to return home, when suddenly out of the bushes someone called her in a hushed voice. Frightened to death, Matronka at first wanted to run away, but, after standing there for a bit, she went toward the voice anyway: and from the darkness her eyes made out a man and woman, totally wet, so that their clothes were stuck to their bodies, as though that had just come out of the water. The woman shivered from the cold or a fever, and the man was making a bed out of branches.

"Good woman, help us if you can. And if you can, take us with you, or tell us where we can hide," having approached Matronka close up, the man spoke in rapid fire. "We are from the other side of the river. From Cheremoshne. The Soviets are deporting entire families of people today. Good woman, they are deporting all the most respectable *gazdas* from the village! They know there that my wife and I escaped to this side. But, I think, they won't get to us. Though your Romanians have some kind of *Geschäft* with them and are selling people. But, if you can, let us stay this night at your place, please take us in."

"We'll take you right away," a quiet, but gravelly man's voice said as though it had leapt onto his shoulders from behind him....

Two Soviet border guards quickly led the three of them onto the other side of the river, further down through the current where there the water was more shallow, sticking them with their rifle butts in the back and with their hands tied behind their backs.

And on this side it was quiet as if it were dead: no wind, no Romanian border guards. Just the water gurgling.

...At first they beat all three of them, not asking anything or listening.

Then they divided them up and beat Matronka alone, now only between interrogations. They asked how long she had known these two OUN[56] members, who had crossed the border, how and when they arranged meetings, how many times they met before that, what kind of information they passed along to one another. Then several times they slowly squashed her fingers between the door and the jamb—and she just held out until she peed from the pain. Then they beat her more—and splashed her with water to bring her to, and then beat her again.

After that they asked her what was happening on the other bank of the river. She told them everything she knew: who was born, who died, how the vegetables were growing, what the names of her neighbors were, how

---

56   The OUN was the Organization of Ukrainian Nationalists.

many soldiers were in the village—but this didn't satisfy the ones who were beating her, and everything started over again.

They locked her up for the night in a cellar without steps, where it was filled with rats scurrying, and there was nothing that you could even lean against. She stood that way the entire night by the wall, from time to time shuffling her beaten legs to chase away the nighttime filth. And from the first light of morning an armed escort silently led Matronka to a similarly empty, but bright, room and left her alone for a long time.

In about an hour an officer entered and in an amiable voice, meant for meeting and not for interrogation, asked Matronka to sit down on a chair that was brought in. Matronka feebly fell onto the chair, placing, however, her hands on her knees.

At first the officer drew the white blinds on the window, locked the door from the inside, and then several times walked around the chair, for a long time examining the woman. Once or twice he silently tugged on her tattered braid, smoothed the hair on her crown, and then grabbed her by the chin:

"I'm not going to beat you. I'm going to ask questions—and you just answer the truth. And then I'll release you. Good?" He looked into her eyes.

Wiping away her welled tears, Matronka nodded her head as a sign of agreement.

"And now tell me, who told you or forced you to go to the pre-arranged place to the river to pick up the fugitives?" With a single finger he pressed the dimple on her chin until she felt pain.

"No one. I was looking for my cow. And they were there already."

"All right. Then tell me the following: is it also you, or those who sent you to the river, who helped two men from our side to hide a week ago?"

"No. I told you: our house is not far from the river, and we graze our livestock in the meadows. I went to drive our cow home. I go to the river every day to herd the livestock. Don't you see that from this side?"

"...Aha, you came every day—and let them know on this side... How did you do this?"

"I didn't let them know anything," Matronka began to cry.

"All ri-ght. You didn't let them know anything. Then why is your bosom wet?"

"My milk leaked. I have a three-month-old child. Let me go, sir... my child is in the house alone and hungry... the milk will dry up...," she again began to cry, wiping her tears with her sleeve. "I don't know anything. I'm telling you the whole truth."

"Aha!" It was as though the officer rejoiced, pulling her hand away from her eyes. "You have a three-month-old child left over there and the milk has been leaking from your breasts! Obviously, you're really juicy. We'll check right now if you're telling the truth.

With those words he bent low over her, sniffed her bosom, then roughly plucked out her blouse from behind her apron skirt, lifted it up to her chin, knelt down and with all his strength with two fingers squeezed at first the bulging nipple of one, and then with his entire hand grabbed the second breast. As if he wanted to milk her to the last drop. Thin squirts splashed into the officer's face—and quicker and quicker, with both his hands, he pressed and released Matronka's breasts that were firmer than even the most respectable maiden, and round like melons, with both his large hands from time to time nestling his face near Matronka's mouth, as though he were trying to bite or kiss her, and she screamed hysterically from the pain in a voice different from her own, because he was squeezing her breasts like cow udders, until she crumpled unconscious onto the floor.

...When she came to her senses, the officer fixed his riding breeches and with satisfaction made a wry face as he wiped away the remains of the breast milk from his face. He spoke slowly and reluctantly, as though he had just been intimate with a woman:

"I'm letting you go just because you have a small child, big breasts, and long hair. And now your cow will be giving me milk instead of you. But remember one thing woman, if you even one time, anywhere to anyone, even to your husband, say what happened to you...."

"I don't remember anything...," Matronka didn't let him finish his sentence and looked into his eyes.

"That's good. A sha-a-rp girl. At night a man from your village will come and accompany you across the water. You'll sit there, where he leaves you until someone finds you. But also forget that man, even if he's a brother to you."

...Dmytro Uhryn accompanied Matronka. He was the one who in a few days would present bread and salt on an embroidered cloth to the German in waxed boots. He didn't say a word to her and didn't look into her eyes.

They crossed the river in the middle of the night, not far from the border post, but for some reason this time no one stopped them, not even the guard, who either was dozing in his sentry box, or was giving the appearance that he was dozing.

And today her tormenter, without recognizing his former victim, pried out of little Darusya the truth of what happened that night....

*

...Uncle Vasyl—her second cousin on her mother's side—looked at Mykhailo both sympathetically and angrily at the same time. He well understood what misfortune had befallen his relative, but he didn't understand what kind of help the latter was asking of the old *gazda*, who owned the mountain valley in Boznya. The mountain valley half belonged to the collective farm, and half—to people, and Uncle Vasyl—was the most senior of them.

For the second day Mykhailo walked from mountain valley to mountain valley, from house to house, begging from people any kind of edible goods, promising to work off what he borrowed in hired labor. And some, who listened him out, helped, because they knew Mykhailo wasn't lying. Some, especially the wealthy *gazdas,* laughed into their moustaches and refused. And then, Mykhailo couldn't say how such a thing happened, but he waited for a bit in the tall grass or near the flocks until he could steal from a conspicuous place at least a fistful of butter or a big jar of sour cream, and then got on his horse. Strange as it was for Mykhailo himself to do that, these individual and completely unnoticeable thefts did not pain his conscience. Though, if you tell the truth, Mykhailo wasn't thinking about conscience then. He knew one thing: either twice the quota of milk products, or Siberia.

However, even what he had stolen or borrowed was far from being enough to cover what the MGB agents were demanding of him.

…And right then Uncle Vasyl waved his open palm right in front of Mykhailo's nose and spattered saliva through his moustache as he spoke:

"You're weak in the head, Mykhailo! How can I just give away the product of the people's work just for free?! Though you're a bit of a relative, you're the kind of family, my man, that it's better not to have one, sorrys for my words. Nothin's the way it's supposed to be… And later, what do I say to the *gazdas*? I understand that the summer is long and you can do yourself in with all the work, but even for you, you know how much you'd need to toil to work off these kind of farm products? And how will I explain to the people, that because of your stupid head they've lost the product of so much work? Does you thinks everyone'll be happy that the work of their hands has gone not to their own storehouse, but into the Soviet procurement facility? Does you thinks others'll be happy their milk has gotten into the hands of the Galician lads? I have little to help you, Mykhailo. I got kids, too, and I want to live till my natural death. In worse times I somehow avoided this misfortune, but I don't want to get involved now.

…Who knows how this one-sided conversation of uncle's would have ended if from the sheepshed there had not emerged a tall man, whom Mykhailo recognized as his nocturnal visitor from Holub's squadron. The man was in his uncle's *keptar*[57] sheepskin coat and a green hat, with a rifle over his shoulder. Mykhailo's breath was taken away.

"*Gazda* Vasyl," Mykhailo's nocturnal visitor addressed the old man, "stop this empty conversation. We'll return to the *gazda* what we took, and we'll work out something with you when the man goes to the village."

"But you'll die of hunger!" Mykhailo unexpectedly for himself interrupted the man. "I won't take it back…."

"If we haven't died in winter, then we won't now for sure," the man from the forest began to laugh, "look what kind of summer is beginning. And God is good. And people will help. You're not the only one who wanted to help us."

"No," Mykhailo sighed. "I'd rather go to Siberia…."

"You can always go to Siberia," the man from the forest gave a whistle. "Take the saddlebag sacks over there with cheese and *brynza* on the horse, and get a move on over to the village while it's not too late."

The horse loaded with full saddlebag sacks walked as though he were carrying a corpse, but Mykhailo didn't spur on the creature. At the moment the horse was kinder to him than people who made a thief out of him. "For the first time in my life I've stolen," Mykhailo thought

---

57   A short sleeveless sheepskin coat worn by the Hutsuls. For a picture of one see: http://uk.wikipedia.org/wiki/%D0%93%D1%83%D1%86%D1%83%D0%BB%D1%8C%D1%81%D1%8C%D0%BA%D0%B8%D0%B9_%D1%81%D1%82%D1%80%D0%96%D0%B9. Or: http://folkcostume.blogspot.ca/2011/03/kyptar-hutsul-sheepskin-vest.html.

195

somewhat indifferently, dragging his hobbled feet behind the horse, not looking to either side or at the road. "I've become a thief—and God is not punishing me. Why?" Mykhailo asked himself, sensing his heart anxiously beating in his chest.

For the first time in several years he felt that he had a heart—and shouted out to the horse "giddy up"....

...Matronka, in a white blouse embroidered for Easter on her naked body, was dangling in the woodshed attached to a girder with her long braid wound around her neck, her black tongue sticking out of her mouth, almost touching the ground with her fingers, with a large puddle beneath her.

Bareheaded, unbraided Darusya with both of her tiny hands held on to her mother's bare and barefoot legs, so that at first two fully-grown men—Mykhailo and Dmytro, the husband of the neighbor Maria—weren't able to drag away the child.

And later, when Didushenko arrived, yet two more men couldn't take down Matronka from the girder, until Didushenko said to cut off her braid....

From that moment on Darusya lost her voice. And in time in Cheremoshne they started calling her sweet.

To this day.

"You see, dearie, how it is in this world... And try to convince me if it's not so. When Mykhailo really loved the late Matronka, forgive her, Lord, for her sins, the village lads called him Dovbush.[58] They said, look, he has one darling, if only he doesn't die because of her. And that's what happened...."

---

58 The Ukrainian outlaw leader Oleksa Dovbush (1700-1745) from the Carpathians, who is often compared to Robin Hood.

"True, but the real Dovbush had more than one darling…."

"You must have been one of Dovbush's darlings since you know how many of them he had…."

"It doesn't matter if I was or wasn't, but the Galicians know more about their Dovbush, and my late husband was from Galicia, and told me all kinds of things."

"Rather than tell you all kinds of things, it'd be better if he mebbe made you more children, dearie, then you wouldn't have to worry 'bout it now, whoever has to shut your eyes when your time comes…."

"Lordy-Lordy… what an awful curse there was on that family, and no one knows, what kind, honey…."

"That's not a curse. Such were the times. Was it just Mykhailo who was run over here by a wagon? Did these and those others force just him to go against his will? But the people are silent—they're fearful to this day… for some it's not advantageous to tell the truth. And it's easier to speak of the dead, 'cause they know there is no one to defend them, and tell the whole truth. Mute Darusya will not really tell the great truth… There was a single smart man who told the truth—Ivan Tsvychok. And Tsvychok is gone. They did Tsvychok in."

"Cross yourselves, children, in the morning and evening cross yourselves, and ask God that such a hard fate passes over you. Now you don't believe in anything. And don't understand anything. But I'll give you an example why you need to listen to old folks now and then. You see, this house from the very beginning was cursed, and those who lived in it remained cursed. Look at what a difficult death Mykhailo's father had. His entire life he floated timber rafts down the river, and the rafts took away his life. And his moth-

197

er? And his mother is cursed. Though people lied about her. Mykhailo's mother was an honest woman. People slandered her. Envy did it all. Human envy is worse than weakness. So it was human envy that did everything. The entire family went to the dogs. No goods, no child, no harmony. No nothing... Just the unfortunate Darusya, who suffers for the sins of everyone in this here world, an orphan."

"You see, Annytsya, it was my mother who still told me, may God grants me health so I could remember that Darusya's mother violated the custom right after the wedding. A married woman should cut her hair after the wedding. A woman, who has a husband, she's no maiden anymore; she braided her hair, and Mykhailo, old folk said, unbraided her hair the way you would a child's. There you have your sin. And a sin—that's a squabble with God. God had to at some time resolve this squabble with himself. She used to stand in front of her house with her unplaited hair, like a witch, and he splits wood and laughs."

"Really, you're telling the truth, sweetie Marika. She squabbled with God Himself. She sometimes used to walk through the village with an uncovered head."

"But, women, she didn't go to church with her head uncovered."

"But she did squabble with God!"

"I'll tell you something, daughter dear, that I haven't said to anyone. But I'll be dying soon, and I must have my say. You remember, it was a few years back when childless Mrs. Kalynyak died? She suffered terribly just before her death— she wasn't able to calm down. That too: all her sins. People's possessions didn't give her an easy death. When they were taking away people into the world from the village before *the war, she did an inspection in all the storerooms—and she gathered things like a poor person by the church on Easter. And those possessions were wept over. Few of those who owned them came back. They all found their death there in the world, and some were not allowed to return, and when it became possible, then there was no one to return. Mrs. Kalynyak didn't have her own children, so she took a foster child for herself. And what do you think, daughter? Mrs. Kalynyak gave her foster child other people's stolen blouses, she thought that people forgot whose blouses they were. The people, maybe, forgot. But God sees and remembers everything. And the foster daughter miscarried all her children before the third month, the way a mare tosses off an unsuitable rider. She was suffering for the sins of the mother that wasn't hers. And she also turned out empty, like a bucket filled with holes, to live out her life.*

And departed Mrs. Kalynyak back then incited me to somethin' stupid. She says, let's go, friend, since we were children we've been friends, let's go and take just the blouses. Anyway their gazdas won't be returning. No one will ever know. She says, there are such blouses, and scarves; righteous God—you'll have three lovers on the side before tomorrow. But God gave me the sense not to go… And I didn't need any lovers on the side."

"…Oh, what bad stuff those Russkies have caused among the people, God forbid!"

"All kinds of things happened, dearie… They've done good and bad. I still remember when the first Russkies arrived in 'forty."

"Dearie, I'll tell you in secret, because I'm already old, so I can now tell all the secrets… Then I'll tell you, dearie,

that those Russkies so nicely asked our women for it, that it was easier to give it to them than refuse. And what do you think—we gave them a bit, 'cause our own won't ask so nice."

"Truth is the truth. And more than one asked me, but just one got it. And the other Russkies, those who came already after the war, already asked for it a lot less. They scared our women more with Siberia... And what were the poor women to do? What, do you really think, that Petriuk, who lives near the forge, is Petriuk's son? Didushenko's from Skapen, may his grave sink all the way to hell, who was vile and killed so many people. And you think, why does the younger Petriuk have a cripple for a child? For his father's sins, Didushenko's. Did he make a cripple just from one here?"

"Grams, what about our sweet Darusya, has she been mute and foolish from birth?"

"Not from birth—from fate. But she's not foolish, granddaughter, people think she's foolish because she's not like everyone else. But I don't think that way... And she's not to blame for anything. That's just her fate. It's too early for you to know yet. You'll grow up—and I'll tell you everything. If I'm still alive...."

"You see, Maria, you know everything here, 'cause you've lived as a neighbor for years... If that Ivan Tsvychok hadn't dressed up in a military uniform and in those riding breeches, everything would have been good."

"Maybe it would have, or maybe it wouldn't. He didn't know. And nobody could have known."

"But someone could have told him. You might have told him, Maria...."

"One can't say everything, even if one could. And no one wants to get mixed up in someone else's life. But on the other hand, look, boys get out of the army, they walk through the village in their military uniform—and Darusya never had any problems with that."

"Yes, but they walked around the village, while Tsvychok stood right in front of her eyes. And he already was like family for her, and she took fright, for sure, from the way he looked. What do you think, for sure, that she recalled that happening to her. And it's too bad... I already was thinkin' that it would be a little easier for a poor girl in her old age with Ivan. But now, an orphan. Who'll look after her when we, Maria, die? The road to Yorchykha's gettin' closer for us.

"Oh, dearie-sweetie, golden Vasyutka... Life is a three-color rose,[59] once my mother-in-law said, may she be granted the heavenly kingdom. But I was young—I was foolish. I was thinking maybe it becomes three-colored in her eyes that she is saying that, or what... And she says: daughter-in-law, you think that the rose is rose-colored. But no. That's why it's called three-color. Life's like that. It will appear black to you, then yellow, and there, look, it's burning red. You never know what color you'll see tomorrow. You hope to see one color, but it shows you a different one. Oh, God has thought long to devise all kinds of punishments for people. Long and well He thought, dearie. And we don't know, for what...."

59　The image suggests the traditional Ukrainian tragicomic folksong "Chervona ruzha troyaka" (Three-color Red Rose), in which a woman, beaten by her drunkard husband, abandons him and her children to go past the Danube.

Acknowledgements

Photos from the private collection of Mykola Salagor of Chernivtsi, Ukraine were used for the cover and design of this book.

An excerpt of the translation of the beginning of the novel appeared first in the journal *Metamorphoses* 20.1 (Spring 2012) and another excerpt under the title "Mykhailo's Miracle: The Main Drama" was initially published in *Trafika Europe* 7 (March 2016).

*

I would have never been able to complete this project without the expertise and efforts of my co-translator Olha Tytarenko. She devoted an immense amount of time copiously combing through my first draft of the translation and caught many of my infelicities. She also shared a significant amount of commentary on cultural and linguistic issues with me.

I also have a great debt of gratitude to Svitlana Bednazh for sharing her expertise with me on numerous parts of the manuscript—and also for her encouragement on the project.

Special thanks to Ludmilla Trigos for doing such a thorough copy-editing of the final version of the translation that helped to smooth out rough edges. It is a much better translation as a result of her expertise and efforts.

I, of course, am responsible for any errors or omissions in the translation.

MN

MARIA MATIOS (Марія Матіос; born 19 December 1959) is a Ukrainian poet, novelist and government official. She was born in the village of Roztoky in the Bukovina region, and presently resides in Kyiv. She authored 19 volumes of fiction and poetry, including the novel *Sweet Darusya* (2003), and the collections of stories titled *The Short Life* (2001) and *Nation* (2002). Her prose works have been translated into German, Russian, Polish, English, Serbian, French, Italian, Hebrew, Croatian, and Belorussian. Matios' novel *Hardly Ever Otherwise* has appeared in Yury Tkacz's English translation with Glagoslav Publishers.

Her first poems were published when she was fifteen years old. In 1992 she published her first prose in Kyiv Magazine. Maria Matios bases her books on the unique experiences of her family, whose roots go back as far as 1790. She was the winner of the "Book of the Year 2004" prize and of the Taras Shevchenko National Award in 2005 (for her novel *Sweet Darusya*).

Since 2012 Matios has been a deputy in the Ukrainian parliament as a member of Vitaly Klitshchko's UDAR Party.

MICHAEL NAYDAN is Woskob Family Professor of Ukrainian Studies at The Pennsylvania State University and works primarily in the fields of Ukrainian and Russian literature and literary translation. He received his BA and MA degrees from The American University and his Ph.D. from Columbia University. He has published over 50 articles on literary topics and more than 80 translations in journals and anthologies. Of his more than 40 books of published and edited translations, some of his most recent include *Nikolai Gumilev's Africa* (Glagoslav Publishers, 2018); Yuri Andrukhovych's cultural and literary essays, *My Final Territory: Selected Essays* (University of Toronto Press, 2018); and Abram Terz's literary essays, *Strolls with Pushkin and Journey to the River Black* (Columbia University Press, 2016).

In 2017 he published his literary essays in Ukrainian translation in the volume, *From Gogol to Andrukhovych: Selected Literary Essays* (Piramida Publishers). He has also published a novel about the city of Lviv *Seven Signs of the Lion* (Glagoslav Publishers, 2016), which also appeared in 2017 in Marianna Prokopovych's Ukrainian translation under the title *Sim znakiv leva* (Piramida Publishers). He has received numerous prizes for his translations including the George S.N. Luckyj Award in Ukrainian Literature Translation from the Canadian Foundation for Ukrainian Studies in 2013.

OLHA TYTARENKO received her BA and MA in English from Ivan Franko National University in Lviv, Ukraine, her MA from The Pennsylvania State University, and her Ph.D. from the University of Toronto with a specialty in Russian literature. She is currently an Assistant Professor of Practice of Russian at the University of Nebraska. With Michael Naydan she has co-translated Iren Rozdobudko's novel *The Lost Button* (Glagoslav Publishers), Abram Terz's *Strolls with Pushkin and Journey to the River Black* (Columbia University Press), Maria Matios' novel *Sweet Darusya: A Tale of Two Villages*, and Yuri Vynnychuk's novel *Tango of Death* (the latter two with Spuyten Duyvil).

CPSIA information can be obtained
at www.ICGtesting.com
Printed in the USA
LVHW100102250322
714308LV00002B/331